XANDER'S CLAIM

Copyright © 2021 by Serpentine Creative LLC

All rights reserved. No part of this book may be reproduced in any manner whatsoever without written permission except in the case of brief quotations embodied in critical articles and reviews.

First Printing, 2021

XANDER'S CLAIM

A Maura's Men Novella

STELLA WILLIAMS
Raw Books Editing

Serpentine Creative LLC

CONTENTS

One
1

Two
9

Three
12

Four
16

Five
22

Six
36

Seven
38

Eight
47

Nine	56
Ten	59
Eleven	64
Twelve	70
Thirteen	78
Fourteen	86
Fifteen	91
Sixteen	97
Seventeen	105

CHAPTER ONE

MacDonald Estate, Scotland, 1968

"I can't live like this," Shane whispered to Xander as they stood waiting for Maura to make her usual grand entrance.

"We'll talk about this later," Xander hissed as Maura strolled in with Claude at her side. He had fresh scratches on his back, and his hardened expression demonstrated that Maura hadn't been easy on him. Not that Maura was easy on anyone. She dismissed Claude with a flick of her wrist. Maura's caramel skin was flawless and youthful despite her advanced years. No one knew exactly how old she was. Still, her regal attitude combined with her references to the birth of the Persian Empire put her at an age well before the birth of Christ.

Maura's ink-black curls were pulled back into a long braid that reached the curve of her lower back. It swung tantalizingly above her round bottom as she crossed the room. Her hips swayed seductively with each step she took. In any other circle, Maura would draw looks of admiration. Still, Xander felt like he would lose what little sustenance he had managed to obtain on his brief scouting mission.

When Xander first met Maura, he was admittedly intrigued by her, and he figured it was her beauty that held him captive those first few months. It wasn't until the real horror of Maura was revealed to him that he tried to rebel.

He thought he could take her himself, but despite her lithe womanly figure, she had the strength of over a hundred men. Her beauty had been the death of them all, Maura's greatest strength and only weakness. Maura couldn't care less about jewels and money; what she wanted was eternal youth and beauty. Even as Vampirism slowed the aging process, it didn't erase it completely. Maura made up for what Vampirism lacked by draining beautiful, young women of their blood and young men of their souls.

Alexander, or Xander as Shane had nicknamed him, was the oldest of the six men she currently kept as her slaves. He was tall and had a warrior's build that had made him somewhat unpopular with the ladies of his day but made him perfect for Maura. She needed a protector as well as someone stocky enough to withstand her abuse, both physically and mentally. There had been one before him, but once he showed signs of aging, he disappeared without a trace. No one knew what became of him, and everyone was afraid to find out.

Maura had no tolerance for the "old and ugly" as she liked to say. Felix had come along shortly after Xander, a dandy of the courts. He allowed Maura access to people of power. Felix was the hardest to read for Xander. He didn't seem to detest Maura as much as Xander, Claude, and Shane, but at the same time, he didn't seem to enjoy being in her presence much either. Maura seemed to like collecting her men in pairs because next she acquired Claude and Owen.

Claude had been a burgeoning industrialist; his family owned a small but lucrative oil field, and he'd had dreams of making a name for himself in New York. Claude had been a womanizer even then, so it wasn't long before he fell into

Maura's clutches. Of all the men, Maura called for him the most when she was in her worst moods. No one knew Owen's story, but out of them all, he actually seemed to enjoy Maura's presence. He had even brought his younger brother Philip into Maura's lair. Xander was sure Owen and his brother had their own private circle in Hell reserved just for them.

Shane had only come just recently. He was Maura's expert on the new free love movement. She had lured him with funding for his experiments on the effects of LSD. Once he found out she was kidnapping young women from the study, he made the mistake of confronting her. She killed him, turned him, and made it impossible to continue his research and free-thinking ways.

Xander could only have described Shane as a lost puppy during his first year of servitude under Maura. He'd tried to maintain his scientific mind, but nothing he could do could prepare him or help him cope with what his life and work had become. There was no way such a free spirit could survive her brutal domination for long. He couldn't deal with Maura and her destructive ways for much longer.

"Owen, you will take Philip to find a few morsels. I'm feeling a little parched," Maura said.

Xander hated the way she always lingered on the 'S' sound. His fangs being larger than hers, he knew it wasn't a matter of speaking around them.

Owen nodded at Maura before making his way out of the room. Xander hated to admit that he relaxed a little at the thought of those two being off the estate. Owen may have no conscience, but at least he was more well-adjusted than his brother. Philip was a little off and spent most of his days locked in his room. He only answered for Maura and Owen.

"My lady," Xander said, approaching Maura, but she put a hand up to stop him.

"Shane will be next. I'm afraid Claude has had his fill," she said.

Xander shot an apologetic look at Shane. It took all Xander had to do nothing as Shane made his way to Maura. Xander fought the anger building inside him as he watched Maura devouring Shane with her black eyes. Maura was indeed without a soul, and those eyes were a dead giveaway. In the past, when she had mingled among humans, she had to have used some magic to make her eyes the sultry caramel brown they had been when Xander first encountered her. A wicked smile graced her full pouty lips as he took her awaiting hand.

"My pleasure as always," Shane chirped, but the tense way he held his body belied his true feelings. Maura was well aware of that fact, but it only heightened her arousal. She gripped his hand tightly, letting Shane know that she was itching for whatever fight he had left to try to resist her will. Her grip felt like it was going to break his hand, but Shane refused to flinch, refused to show her she was hurting him. Shane prayed silently that he survived this encounter as Maura led him down the stairs to her chambers. He had to endure for the plan to work.

As soon as Maura disappeared with Shane, Claude collapsed to the floor. If anyone other than Xander had been in the room, he would have held on longer. At least until he got to his room.

"Curse that wretched whore," Xander said, helping Claude to his feet.

He checked the hallway before dragging Claude's deadweight to his room before the others were back to see him in his weakened state.

"I just need a moment," Claude said when Xander put him in his bed.

"No, it can wait until you are better," Xander said, but Claude shook his head.

"I think she knows we aren't under her spell anymore. She was much worse than usual," he said, barely above a whisper. He was so weak.

"You don't have the strength. You need more than a minute to recover. A whole night won't have you fully recovered," Xander said.

"But Shane will be killed with the mood she is in. He hasn't acquired his full power as a Vampire yet," Claude said, and Xander cursed.

"Fine, we will go forward with the plan," Xander said and left the room. He needed to take extra precaution with both Claude and Shane weakened by Maura's sexual deviances. One thing about the plan hadn't changed: Maura would die, even if he had to give his own life to accomplish it.

* * *

Forty Years Later...

"Alright, everyone, let's wrap it up for the day," Professor Felix Aiken called out to his team. A group of twenty students all nodded and went about the daily clean-up of the site. Felix tried his best to keep the team from getting too far with the dig, stalling as best he could. No one could find Maura's corpse. It would garner too much attention and way too many questions.

When Alexander drained the last of her blood, her body had shriveled and become disfigured, her fangs jutting awkwardly from her skull. Luckily for Felix, being an expert on the MacDonald estate and its lore, he was the first pick to lead the excavation. If only he could stall his eager volunteers long enough for funding of the excavation to run out—only then would Maura's grave be safe once again.

Felix took a moment to look out around the grounds. In a way, it was fitting that Maura be buried here. It was her favorite property. Modeled after the famous Stirling Castle, it fit with her delusions of being royalty. Although there was only one main building to the estate, the original owner had been paranoid enough to not only build a wall around the grounds but also to create a network of tunnels that suited Maura's nocturnal lifestyle perfectly.

The house above had been normal enough to fool any passing visitor, but it was in the tunnels and rooms below that all the depravity had occurred. It was the few remains of dungeons and torture devices that had been unearthed that kept the estate in the spotlight. Everyone wanted to know if there was any truth to the rumors.

If only they knew the truth. They couldn't ever know the truth, which is why Felix was so dedicated to his task of keeping his inquisitive students from uncovering what the world was undoubtedly not prepared to handle. The frosty weather had provided a convenient and natural impediment to their progress.

Most of the students enjoyed the leisurely pace that Felix had set for the dig. All but Declan Murray; he was a particular thorn in Felix's side. Even now, Declan was glaring across the site at Felix, obviously upset because the day had been called early. Felix pretended not to notice, but he had his eyes on Declan. Sooner or later, his eagerness to complete this excavation might get him in a lot more trouble than he bargained for. Felix sealed the envelope containing news of his progress with the dig. He would mail it to Alexander first thing tomorrow. It was nearly time for them to rotate posts, but Felix wasn't ready to step away from everything just yet.

* * *

Declan Murray fought back his frustration with Professor Aiken's lack of urgency. Could he not see that they were on the brink of a significant discovery? As soon as Declan had read about the secret passage found under the MacDonald estate, he knew that there was considerable history to be discovered and possibly even treasure. The MacDonald estate had an exciting history with stories equally as disturbing as Dracula's castle but from a much earlier time. There were many folk tales about young women being lured there by handsome young men and never being seen again, rumors of shadowy figures and screams in the night; it was the stuff of horror stories and history gold.

Declan's family had originally come from the village just south of the estate, so he had grown up hearing the tales of the MacDonald estate. The most interesting and exciting of them were those of the lady of the manor, how she never seemed to age, and neither did the young men she kept in her presence. It was these family tales that had Declan dreaming of the fountain of youth. Declan had hopes that this passage would lead to the famed fountain and possibly other more tangible treasures. Reluctantly, Declan started packing his things. If the excavation didn't begin progressing soon, Declan just might have to take matters into his own hands. He smiled at the thought of discovering the fountain all on his own, without having to share the glory. Would he drink the water, or just bottle it up and sell it to others who thirsted for a little more to life? Two more days and he would surely find out.

CHAPTER TWO

Shane cautiously entered the study where Xander sat reading what appeared to be an intense letter, judging by the furrow of his brow. If it were any other night or for any other reason, Shane would be a lot more comfortable with approaching him, but tonight was anything but usual. It was the anniversary of their freedom. The night Xander, Claude, Felix, and Shane had risen against and defeated Maura.

It was usually a night of reflection and private celebration as well as a night of mourning, all of them sharing stories about their lives before Maura had taken control of them. Tonight, however, was different. Tonight, Shane would be embracing his new life, moving on for the sake of love.

Shane was taking a significant risk by asking Xander to accompany him on a double date with Molly and Cat. In any other circumstance, Claude would have been the better choice. He was a serious lady's man, as demonstrated multiple times over the years Shane had known him. Claude was also quite the chauvinist and was not the person Shane could see making small talk with two modern women. Xander wasn't much better a choice in that regard, but he at least wouldn't be as outright rude as Claude could be.

"Do you need anything?" Xander asked, looking up from his reading. Shane smiled, trying to act casual.

"I have a proposition for you," Shane began, but Xander put his hand up, stopping him mid-sentence.

"I'm not interested," Xander said, and Shane sighed.

"You don't even know what I was going to ask," he protested, but Xander only shook his head. Folding the letter, he stood, putting it back in its envelope before locking it in his personal drawer of the desk.

"I don't have to. I know you much too well. You are nervous, meaning it's something I won't agree to easily, and tonight I am feeling rather disagreeable," Xander said and left the room. Shane took a deep breath and followed.

"It's just one night in the company of two amazing women. You have already met Molly, and her friend is a really nice person," Shane said, trying not to wince at his little lie about Cat. Cat was a nice person—you just had to get past a few quirks first.

"I can smell your desperation, but you know my policy on dealing with outsiders, especially women," Xander said and stalked up to his room.

"Did I hear mention of women?" Claude asked, making his presence known.

Shane rolled his eyes before smiling. Claude had stepped in after overhearing Xander's adamant refusal, and since it was the last minute, Shane hadn't had a choice.

It was either bring Claude along or disappoint Molly. Xander was a lost cause, but Claude wasn't one to turn away a chance to mingle with women. He did his best to bring Claude up to speed on his situation without going into too much detail. The problem was when Shane spoke of Molly, he couldn't help but be as flowery and generous as her personality.

"Together forever? Is this girl serious?" Claude laughed, earning a glare from Shane.

"Watch how you talk about my girlfriend," Shane growled, but Claude just shrugged.

"So, is this friend some beastly brute, or is she just desperate? I can do desperate," Claude said.

Shane instantly regretted asking Claude to come along. He had tried his best to get Xander to come, but out of the three of them, Xander was definitely the least willing to take a chance on love. It was an old story that, despite their closeness, Xander never shared.

Besides, maybe Cat was just the medicine Claude needed. She was harsh and sarcastic and wouldn't put up with his egomania. Shane knew precisely how much Cat was dreading this double date, but, like Cat, he would do anything for Molly. The night was definitely not going to be boring.

CHAPTER THREE

"I never thought together forever would be literal," Molly gushed, stars in her eyes as she performed the last of her pre-date ritual.

"Molly, I love you, and Shane is awesome, but are you sure this is a good idea?" Cat asked her best friend since middle school.

Molly glared at her in the mirror before setting down her brush, her auburn hair flowing perfectly straight over her delicate shoulders. In school, Cat had been the only person not to tease Molly about her ginger curls with matching freckles. It was how they had become such good friends. Molly and Cat had been misfits together.

A twist of fate and a change of county lines had put Molly's new foster home and Cat's neighborhood within the richest and whitest of school districts. Cat had been happy to finally go to a school that gave her choices as far as academics and took full advantage from day one. Yet, despite everything good that came with the change, Cat had been forced to scare a few people in order to make life bearable.

It had been an awkward transition for Cat, going from the bullied to the bully. To this day, it still frustrated Cat that before Molly, she'd been typecast because of her brown skin and less than affluent background. Molly had been too weak to make her own place in the new environment. At first, Cat ignored it, choosing to stay out of things she didn't feel concerned her. However, Cat's conscience had gotten the better of her when she ran across Molly being dragged by her hair by a girl from school.

After seeing Molly so tormented, she decided to take her under her protection. Molly had already been self-conscious about her hair before they called even more attention to it. She eventually came to terms with her riotous hair, but on special occasions, she relished the three-hour process of taming it into a sleek straight style.

"I'm not saying you have to spend forever with whoever Shane brings, but wouldn't it be nice for us to be able to stay friends forever?"

"Of course, it would, sweetie, but this isn't Twilight, and regardless of whether we both live forever or not, you will always be my best friend for life. I mean, seriously, I already have the tattoo," Cat replied, flashing the tacky 'best friend' heart on her hip with Molly's name.

Molly sported a similar heart with Cat's name on her hip. It had been a drunken decision after commiserating the break up with Molly's ex-boyfriend, Hank. The only good thing that had come out of that night had been meeting Shane. After getting the tattoos at some shady downtown shop, Shane had saved them from the improper advances of the bikers from the bar next door. Molly had shamelessly thrown herself at Shane that night, but he'd been a complete gentleman, making sure that they made it home safely even after she had vomited on his shoes. Molly had been so appalled by her behavior that night it took Shane two months to convince her to go on a date with him.

If Shane hadn't made it a point to be friends with Cat while their relationship had been in its infant stages, Cat would have been a lot less accepting of the fact that he was a Vampire. Cat always knew something was off with Shane, but she had assumed that he was just a hippie throwback. Seriously, he may have been dressed in today's fashion that first night, but he drove an old Volkswagen Beetle and only listened to music from the '60s and early '70s. Not only that but watching 'That 70's Show' with him was painful, as he felt the need to explain all the social nuances at play for each episode. In the end, it all came down to one thing. No matter who or what Shane was, he made Molly happy, and that was all Cat could really ask for her best friend.

Molly grinned from ear to ear before grabbing her purse.

"Shane will be here any moment," she said, completely ignoring the look of pure dread on her best friend's face. Cat sighed heavily when the doorbell rang as if on cue.

"Let's get this over with," she grumbled and stalked to the door. Molly rushed to Shane, throwing her arms around him. Seeing Molly and Shane together was proof positive to Cat that true love did exist. Shane and Molly were lost in their own world as Molly filled Shane in on her day as if they hadn't seen each other in ages. Cat was forced to remind them of her presence by clearing her throat.

"Evening Cat," Shane greeted her with his usual grin, although the apology was evident in his eerily blue eyes.

Cat looked him over. "You didn't get all the grave dirt off," she said as she brushed imaginary dirt from his shoulder.

"I see you are in good spirits," Shane said, his smile never wavering. Cat knew full well he didn't sleep in a grave, but she loved teasing him with all the Vampire clichés. It was how she coped with her best friend falling in love with one.

"Ah, you are an expert," Cat grinned before turning her attention to Claude, "and you would be my Edward."

Shane choked back a laugh while Molly glared. Claude frowned, not getting the reference. Being from the Industrial Era, his fascination had always been in the advances of science and technology, not in keeping up with popular cinema.

"My name is Claude," Claude said, taking Cat's hand. He placed a gentle kiss across her fingers, his eyes never leaving hers. Cat snorted and snatched her hand away.

"This is not a supermarket. No free samples here, buddy," she said and crossed her arms over her chest before walking out the door. Molly shot an apologetic look at Claude, and the remaining trio followed Cat to Shane's car.

"Okay Dracula, let's hit the road," Cat said once everyone was situated in the car. This favor was definitely one Cat was never going to let Molly forget.

CHAPTER FOUR

Declan waved to his roommate as he headed out for the night. The idiot really thought he would be staying in while the rest of the group was out drinking, but Declan had other plans. He was tired of waiting for those lushes to get on board with speeding up the dig. It was time he took action on his own. They were close—he knew it, and he knew Professor Aiken knew it too. What Declan didn't understand was why Aiken seemed to become more agitated the closer they got to reaching what looked to be the first major room along the passage they had uncovered so far.

Declan could have sworn there was a wooden structure in the area he had been digging. Professor Aiken had dismissed it and had suggested they go over an area that made no sense to any seasoned archaeologist or historian. As soon as Declan was sure his roommate was well on his way, he grabbed his bag of tools and headed out the door. Tonight, he was going to see exactly what he had found.

* * *

Felix's senses were on red alert. He tried to stay focused on the crowd of students around him, but he couldn't help but notice that Declan wasn't amongst them. Not that Declan was really sociable with the others; it just wasn't like him not to come at all. He usually showed up for a drink or two before finding a young woman to enjoy the night with. Perhaps he was just running a little late or had gone to a different pub. There were lots of other bars for him to be unwinding in. Even so, something was just not right. Felix downed the last of his drink and headed to the door. He was so preoccupied with his thoughts. He almost knocked down a young woman on his way out.

* * *

It hadn't taken Declan long to find where he'd left off earlier in the day. Still, it seemed someone had heaped new mud on top of it, obliterating his previous recovery work. The delay had been frustrating but minimal.

"I knew it!" he exclaimed in a whisper.

Declan finished brushing the last of the dirt from the sturdy wooden door he had only managed to get a glimpse at before. He did a little dance of excitement and rubbed his hands together before attempting to push the door open. He hoped it wouldn't give him much trouble. There was a genuine possibility that the other side was filled in with dirt as well, but he was sure he had felt air coming from the seam of the door as he uncovered it.

Declan gave the door a tentative push and pull, and surprisingly, it swung open without much effort. As if it had been fully functioning just yesterday instead of hundreds of years prior. For a moment, Declan felt disappointed. Maybe this was just a failed root cellar—nothing as old or as important as it had seemed in the daylight.

He peered inside, seeing nothing at first, but the smell of decay that hit him immediately had him stumbling back. He tripped over his still open tool bag, sending him sprawling into the dirt. He was stunned for a moment but propped himself up. Cursing, he crawled forward in search of his flashlight that had rolled into the musky cavern. He inched along, running his hands against the smoothed dirt floor, occasionally touching what felt like shards of bone.

With how his luck was going so far, maybe he'd stumbled on an old dog kennel or perhaps a crypt judging by the smell. Finally, his hand came in contact with cool metal. He grinned, wrapping his hands around the familiar shape of his flashlight. Declan started to stand but thought better of it at the last second. He didn't know how high the ceiling was, and the last thing he needed was to get knocked unconscious due to carelessness. He'd come too far for that.

Declan got back on all fours and turned back towards the entrance. He was far enough inside the room that all he could see of the entrance was just a sliver of slightly brighter darkness. He was only a few feet away when he felt a hand on his ankle and froze, struggling with his flashlight. What he saw had him dropping it again. A blood-curdling scream escaped him before he felt the stab of fangs on his leg.

* * *

Felix began to run as soon as he heard the screams. He was suddenly glad he hadn't slacked off on his guard duties any more that night. Felix raced to the dig site, but it was too late; Declan's body lay lifeless at the entrance of Maura's now uncovered tomb. A chill ran over Felix as he cautiously crept closer. He bent down and checked his neck; there were no marks. Relief washed over Felix as his fears were put to rest. This couldn't possibly have been Maura's doing. This was something he could handle and turn over to the human authorities, but just to be sure, he wanted to move Maura's remains.

He and the others had planned to move her remains to a better location long ago, but expedience and other factors had waylaid that. The opening of MacDonald Estate to archaeological research had been one of those factors.

Felix stood, picking up Declan's discarded flashlight as he entered the dark room. He swung the light across the floor, spotting what he expected: to the right of the room lay the dried bones of Owen and Philip. They had been defanged prior to being killed, so Felix had nothing to worry about from those two. When he swung the light to the left, instead of the twisted flesh jerky he expected to see, stood Maura, haggard and old, but alive, with flames of hell and damnation flickering in her soulless black eyes. Fresh blood dripped from one corner of her mouth, and Felix's gaze flicked over to where Declan's body lay, only to see it beginning the stages of change.

"No," Felix said, but it was too late. Maura attacked, and despite her weakened state, she quickly overpowered him.

"You betrayed me," she snarled before he felt the pierce of her fangs. Felix was immobilized as she drank from him. He could only hope she drained him quickly, but as he felt her tugging at the last of his life, she pulled away, a cruel grin spread across her face.

"Let me," a hoarse but familiar voice said, and Declan came into Felix's view, a fanged smile on his face.

* * *

Xander stood on the balcony outside of his room, looking out at the bright lights of the city below. There was something not right about the air, and he just couldn't shake the feeling that something significant was about to happen. Xander was not one for surprises, and whatever came of this eerie feeling was not welcome. He could not be less excited about it. It was a night like this one that had changed his life forever. A night like this that had stolen his one true love and turned him into someone he barely recognized. A night like this that he had realized what kind of monster he had truly become.

Xander closed his eyes and sighed, taking a sip from his goblet of blood. Not the kind that came from bags and tasted like a sour ale but the good stuff. The black-market stuff he purchased solely for special occasions and nights like this. He didn't ask how the supplier got it, and he didn't want to know. Sometimes ignorance was bliss.

Felix's letter had held nothing but good news. He had even asked to extend his time guarding Maura's tomb for a few more years. Yet Xander still worried. Maybe he should have accepted Shane's offer. It had been far too long since he had set foot off the grounds or even thought of anything other than the past. Shane, being the youngest, had kept his love of life and made it a point to keep up with the times.

No matter how much he tried to convince Shane to limit his contact with the outside world, he never listened. Sure, there were valid reasons to interact outside of the mansion. Like procuring food and making sure, they were still in good standing with the Vampire Council, but those duties were typically left to Xander. Claude could care less, and Shane was not good with negotiating.

Xander had been furious when he first found out about Shane's relationship with a human. It was only after Shane had insisted he met the girl that Xander relented. Seeing the love between them that he had been forced to give up, Xander hadn't had the heart to deny them a happy life together.

CHAPTER FIVE

"I can't believe Molly talked you into taking us to dinner," Cat whispered to Shane. They had just settled into their reserved table at one of the fanciest restaurants in town. Shane shrugged and picked up a menu like he had every intention of ordering.

"It's the least I can do. She wanted her last night to be special," Shane whispered back.

Cat choked on the sip of water she had just taken. Claude slapped her on the back roughly until her sputtering stopped.

"Are you okay?" Molly asked, concern on her face.

"Yeah, I'm fine," Cat said, glaring at Shane.

"So, how much do you know about us?" Claude asked, taking Cat's attention away from Shane for a moment.

"About you? Nothing," Cat said.

"About my kind," he clarified with a smirk.

To any other woman, it would probably have been sexy the way he bantered easily with her, but Cat was not impressed. She could smell the expensive scent of privileged chauvinist all over this one. It was one she had learned well over the years.

"Assholes?"

Cat fought the urge to gloat when he raised an eyebrow at her response. It may have been childish, but hopefully, he finally got the hint. Cat was not interested in the least.

Earlier, her attitude had seemed cheeky and cute. Now it

was just plain annoying. None of his efforts to start a conversation during the thirty-minute drive to the restaurant had been successful. He had tried all his usual tricks, and Cat had seen right through him. Claude wasn't used to a woman being immune to his ample charm and male beauty. Not even her pretty face and curvaceous body could make up for her salty demeanor.

"You know exactly what I mean," he clipped out, unable to contain his annoyance.

Cat smiled smugly.

"Enough," she said and picked up her own menu.

Cat hadn't forgotten Shane's comment about tonight being Molly's last. She couldn't believe Molly wouldn't have told her about it before this train wreck had started. Cat had every intention of bringing it up with them both, sooner rather than later. The waiter arrived to take their order, postponing further discussion for a moment.

Cat couldn't help but roll her eyes as Molly ordered nothing more than a chicken salad and water with lemon. Leave it to Molly to hold to a diet when she was obviously planning on giving up real food for the rest of her existence. Shane didn't even seem fazed as he ordered the same. Shane had explained to Cat that Vampires could eat food; it just wasn't necessary. The sense of taste faded, and food lost its appeal a few years after being turned.

"The lady will have the same," Claude ordered for Cat, which earned him yet another glare.

Cat would have said something if he hadn't ordered her exactly what she had been planning on ordering herself.

"I'm going to the ladies' room before the food arrives," Molly said.

Cat rushed to follow; not only was she anxious to get away from Claude, but she needed to clarify a few things with Molly first.

"Why didn't you tell me you were eloping?" Cat said as soon as they were in the restroom. Eloping had become their code word for Molly being turned. It came in handy when discussing her relationship with Shane in public.

"I thought you understood that this was meant to be a celebration," she said.

Cat rolled her eyes.

"I think you are rushing things. Why does it have to be now? Can't you wait a few more years?"

Molly frowned.

"If I wait any longer, I'll look more like Shane's mother than his girlfriend," she whined, stretching out invisible wrinkles in the mirror.

"That's not such a big deal. Cougars are really in right now," Cat rationalized.

Molly wasn't budging.

"I understand you are worried, and I love you for it, but Shane makes me happy. I'm ready to give myself to him, fully," she said. The look in her eyes had Cat's defenses falling even if the icky feeling in her stomach didn't go away.

The rest of the dinner went relatively smoothly, despite the obvious tension amongst the group. Molly did her best to try to help Cat find common ground with Claude; she was ever the hopeful one. It was one of the things that Cat loved most about her since Cat was more of the glass-half-empty type. Shane eventually distracted her, and Claude decided it was best to make minimal conversation. The outcome was a very quiet dessert for Cat, even if she couldn't quite enjoy it. The closer it came to the end of the evening, the closer it was to the end of her best friend, and Cat was definitely not looking forward to that.

"Thank God that's over," Cat sighed as they pulled out of the restaurant parking lot. Cat was anxious to get home. She was choosing not to think about what would be going on after that.

"Not quite," Claude grimaced as he pointed at the road sign. They weren't going back in the direction of the house.

"Where are we going?" Cat asked, and Molly turned around in her seat to face Cat.

"I wanted you to be there even if you aren't going to be joining us," she said.

Cat shook her head.

"No way! I'm not going to watch them kill you," Cat yelled.

Shane looked over his shoulder at her. It was only a split second that his eyes were away from the road, but it was just long enough for the car to drift into oncoming traffic. Then everything went black.

* * *

Xander woke with a start. Something wasn't right. There was a new presence in the house—a female presence. He knew Shane had planned on turning Molly last night, but the mood in the house was not right as Xander made his way into the kitchen. The three of them - Shane, Claude, and Xander—usually shared a glass of blood after waking each night, but tonight he only found Claude looking drained and somber.

"What happened?" Xander asked, instantly concerned.

"I made a mistake," Claude half-whispered before getting up and walking out the room.

Xander followed him. Claude wasn't the cryptic type. He was the most straightforward, in your face, person Xander had ever met. Claude disappeared into his room, but Xander stopped dead in his tracks at the door. Now he saw what had Claude so out of sorts.

The woman looked so innocent and helpless, lying lifeless on Claude's bed. Her clothes were torn and bloody, and dark bruises covered her body. Xander found himself standing directly above her, appalled by what he was seeing.

"What the hell happened?" he growled, and Claude flinched.

"Molly's gone," Shane said from the far corner of the room.

Xander had been so transfixed by the woman and the state she was in; he hadn't realized Shane was in the room. His clothes were torn and covered in blood, but otherwise, he looked fine, physically at least. What scared Xander was the deadness of his eyes. It was something Xander hadn't seen since they had broken Maura's thrall over them. The devastation he heard in his friend's voice was something all too familiar. Molly was dead. Shane had lost the woman he loved and with her, his hope.

* * *

Cat was in severe pain as she lay on the softest thing she'd ever felt. Her entire body was on fire, and she was sure she had several broken bones. The movement wasn't on her list of priorities at the moment, however, Cat decided opening her eyes might be a good idea. Anything to erase the images of her best friend lying decapitated next to her on the road. Horror had never been her thing. Cat wasn't expecting anything extraordinary, maybe a few blank walls or some kind of art to be in her line of sight. Instead, she was startled by the presence of the most gorgeous male specimen she had ever laid eyes on.

He was tall. Well, she was still lying down, and her vision wasn't exactly clear. Her eyes were sore and practically swollen shut, but she knew he was tall. Tall enough that his hair brushed the doorjamb as he stood in the door. Not only that, but he was definitely built. His arms and chest bulged in his button-down shirt, and he wasn't even flexing. Cat was sure he had a matching six-pack hidden under there. His face was all angles and symmetrical perfection, from his sandy brown locks and stern hazel gaze to the press of his full, kissable lips. He looked pissed and concerned and incredibly hot. Too bad those soulful eyes were trained on something other than her.

* * *

Xander turned his attention back to the woman on the bed. He was struck by her beauty even with all the damage from whatever accident that had occurred. He studied her as she lay there. Her hair was dark and plastered to her head with blood and who knew what else. Even so, he could imagine how it would look brushing her shoulders, framing her oval face, and accenting her high cheekbones.

Her eyes were almond-shaped. He could tell even with the swelling and bruising of the black eyes she was sporting. Her full bottom lip was split and bleeding, and Xander had to clench his fists at his sides to keep from touching them and tasting her. This was not suitable. It had been way too long since Xander was in the presence of a woman, let alone an extremely attractive one. He was appalled that he was lusting after a battered woman, no matter how beautiful she was.

* * *

As much grief and confusion were coursing through her brain, Cat should have felt distressed at her current situation. It was the sight of this gorgeous warrior man, standing over her like he was her own personal guard, that made her feel just a little piece of calm. Cat held on to that feeling as tight as she could before she gave in to the exhaustion claiming her body and mind.

The man stayed in her dreams, guiding her through the next few torturous days as her body healed. This may not be the journey Cat had planned for her life, but she was glad she had someone there to ground her and give her purpose when all she felt was loss and confusion.

Cat woke up again, this time to a more familiar face standing over her: Shane. At least she was sure it was Shane. The man was almost sickly pale with dark circles under his eyes, but it was most definitely Shane. He looked as if all the joy had been sucked from him, but when he saw that Cat's eyes had opened, he knelt down to her. Just a small glimmer of something registered in his eyes before they became dead again, and

Cat wanted to cry as memories flooded her head. Molly was gone, and she was a Vampire.

"Good evening, Cat," Shane half-whispered, and Cat threw her arms around him in a hug. She wasn't surprised when he flinched a little.

Although they had grown close before the accident, Cat had never felt comfortable with this level of physical affection. Any other circumstance would have been better than this, however, and Cat had a feeling they both needed a good hug. Shane probably needed it more than she did. After a few moments, she let him go and released the breath she hadn't known she had been holding.

"Awesome! She's awake," a vaguely familiar voice said from behind Shane.

They both turned to see Claude leaning in the doorway, a mug in his hand. He smiled and crossed the room, handing Cat the mug. Cat felt thirsty, so she grabbed it from him and took a big gulp only to feel sick immediately after.

"What the hell?"

Cat grimaced as she noticed the fingers she had wiped her mouth with were smeared with blood.

"Yeah, bagged blood does taste awful, but it helps us blend in with society, so you'll have to get used to it," Claude said.

Cat glared at him. She hadn't liked him at their first meeting, and now she was confident he would not be one to grow on her either.

"She just woke up. Give her some space," Shane said, pushing Claude back.

Cat was grateful, but she still had a lot of questions that needed answering, and Claude seemed a lot more forthcoming than Shane at the moment. Cat looked at the remaining blood in the mug and took a deep breath before chugging the last of it, careful not to breathe through her nose as she drank. It was a technique she had learned doing shots in college. Not breathing helped to not taste it.

"Still horrendous. I think I'll stick with real food for a while longer," she said and handed Shane the mug.

"Since you have eaten, I guess it's time I show you around the house," Shane said, making a sweeping gesture with his arm.

The tour was shorter than Cat had expected. Granted, Cat had expected Shane to live in some huge castle-like mansion. At least that was how Molly had described it after her visit. Sharp pain sliced through her at the reminder of her friend. It shouldn't be Cat here with Shane. It should have been Molly. Yet, she could hardly be disappointed with the smaller mansion he shared with two other Vampires. Claude, she knew already, but the third didn't seem interested in meeting her fresh out of the grave.

"So how long before I can go home?" Cat asked, and the smile Cat had managed to coax out of Shane faltered.

"I'm afraid there is nothing for you to go back to. It's been nearly a week since the accident. They believed you dead at the scene," Claude said, and Shane glared at him.

"We have put your belongings in storage. When you are stronger, I'll help you go through it all to see what you would like to bring here," Shane said, and she rolled her eyes.

"Bring here? I can't have my own place?" Cat asked, and Shane shook his head.

"For now, it's safer if you remain with us," Shane said.

"Yes. As your sire, it's my duty to protect and train you," Claude said.

Cat began to feel sick again at the reminder that her life had taken an unexpected and unwanted turn. It was all too much—she needed air as she suddenly felt suffocated. She excused herself and made her way down the hall to where she remembered the bathroom to be. She made it halfway there, only to slip into a side door when she was sure no one was looking. The room she entered was some kind of study. At the far side of the room was a set of double doors leading to a balcony. She crossed the room and exited through the doors. Cat welcomed the blast of crisp, frozen air that hit her face. She wasn't typically a winter person, but the fresh air was exactly what she needed. Maybe the chill would wake her from this nightmare.

There was a light layer of ice on the balcony, so she was careful as she edged her way out onto it. From the balcony, she could see across the relatively small yard to an impressive view of the city below. It gave the illusion of being on top of the world, so to speak. Cat sighed as her imagination began to wander. She imagined being a princess at a ball. Bored with the politics inside, she had escaped watching several lovers scattered throughout the gardens. She watched them enjoying each other, thinking they were hidden from view. After a few moments, Cat shook her head, clearing away the nonsense.

It took Disney almost 80 years to make a black princess and Cat only two seconds. Her imagination hadn't gotten the best of her like that in a long time. Fairy tales didn't exist and neither did fairy tale love. If it did exist, then what happened to Shane and Molly would never have been. Passion was real, passion Cat had known, but love was elusive.

Every girl grows up with the stories of fairy tale princesses finding love and happily ever after by their eighteenth birthday. To Cat, it was one social norm she hoped someone would break someday. Those stories made love seem so easy, and yet, for her, it wasn't. Even her friends from high school could claim to have been in love at least once by now, but not Cat. Maybe she was like the evil stepsisters in the Cinderella story and just wasn't made for true love.

"You shouldn't be out here," a deep, lightly accented voice said.

Startled, Cat turned too quickly, slipping on the ice-covered balcony.

She would have fallen, but the man caught her in his arms. Cat's body pressed close to his. Heat instantly rushed through her, and arousal seeped from her core. She gasped at her body's instant response and looked up to see who was causing it.

"You," she said to the man who had been standing over her the first time she had opened her eyes. His hazel eyes seemed to see straight through her as he set Cat to her feet and took a step back.

"You shouldn't be out here," he repeated more sternly, and Cat scowled at him.

"I'm perfectly fine here," she spat, choosing to focus more on the outrage of him telling her where she could and could not be more than on the way her body was reacting to his.

* * *

Xander scowled back at the woman he hadn't been able to keep out of his mind since he laid eyes on her. As soon as he had realized she was awake, he made it a point to keep away, then she had walked into his study, ruining whatever chance he had of forgetting about her. She definitely had to go. Roughly, he took Cat's arm, trying not to notice as she winced. Her bruises must not have completely healed yet. He stopped and loosened his grip just a little, aware that he wasn't very gentlemanly.

* * *

Cat saw anger flash across his face before his stone mask slipped back in place. Further confirmation that fairy tales were tragic lies. As dreams became a reality, her knight in shining armor had truly been a beast.

"You will come with me," he practically growled as he dragged her from the balcony. His grip was more gentle but still firm enough to make her follow. Cat managed to get a fix on her body's reaction to this behemoth of a man before she was deposited in front of Shane once again. They were now in the kitchen, which Cat had only gotten a brief glimpse of during the tour.

"Good! I see you have met Xander," Shane said, handing Cat another mug of blood.

"Not so much met as manhandled by," she ground out, glaring at Xander before turning back to Shane.

Claude's mouth tipped in amusement before he took a sip of his own glass.

"I trust he was gentle with you," he said.

Cat gaped at him. If it had been any other person, Cat

would have thrown a fit as well as her fists, but for once in her life, she decided to try and go with the flow. She was, after all, dealing with three experienced Vampires.

"Close your mouth," Xander demanded, going as far as to put a finger under her chin and close it for her. She glared at him, but he just smirked, throwing her off balance. Anytime he showed any emotion other than that expressionless mask, it did things to her insides that Cat didn't want to think about.

"How dare you?" she began, but he put a strawberry in her mouth.

"That's better. At least now you have a reason for your mouth to move so much," he said, and Claude had the nerve to laugh.

As much as she wanted to spit the strawberry out in his face, she didn't want to taste the blood she was drinking. The strawberry was completely clearing her mouth of the coppery blood, so she chewed slowly, glaring at him the entire time. Cat took another sip of blood to wash it down and grimaced. The blood was even more bitter after the super sweet strawberry. She swallowed a few times and tried it again, but this time Claude tipped the mug, forcing her to drink the whole thing.

"There is no need to be forceful. She would have finished it," Shane said

He handed Cat a towel to wipe her mouth.

"The faster she learns how to do things our way and is away from here, the safer she will be," Xander said.

Both Claude and Shane scowled at him. Xander gave them both a pointed look before leaving the room.

"What did he mean by safer?" Cat asked.

Claude looked like he was going to answer, but Shane shot him a look. Cat didn't like the secretive vibe she was getting from the three of them, but for now, she would let it go.

CHAPTER SIX

Maura could barely contain her impatience as she waited for Declan to come to her. She knew he was in the house and could practically feel his excitement. Either he was really looking forward to pleasuring her, or he'd finally accomplished his first task.

"Have you found them?" Maura asked as soon as Declan entered her chambers.

He nodded, taking his clothes off as he joined her on the bed.

"All three are living together in America," he said, trailing kisses up her legs. Declan had to admit that he had been disgusted by her at first, but after luring a few young women into her clutches, she had become the most beautiful and captivating woman he had ever met. He now knew why there had been so many bone shards in the root cellar where he had found her. It also helped that she shared his love for rough sex. Maura held him at bay with a foot on his collar bone.

"Anything else?" she asked.

He sighed, hating and loving that she wasn't allowing him to give her the pleasure he knew she wanted and would soon demand from him.

"The one you call Shane had a lover. I thought we could use her. I looked into it but found that she died in an accident.

The exciting thing—she was the only one found on the scene, but her friend went missing that same night," he said.

Maura got a gleam in her eye.

"Have they buried her yet?" she asked.

Declan shrugged, which earned him a knee to the face. Blood gushed from his nose, and he snarled before biting into her ankle. Maura moaned, her body relaxing a little, and Declan took the opportunity to surge up and sink his teeth where he really wanted to. Maura rocked against him digging her nails into his shoulder.

"Find out if she has been buried yet. She may still be useful," Maura gasped.

Declan nodded sharply, his teeth still tearing at her feminine flesh. He had every intention of obeying Maura's order, but only after he was done with her. Her continued to feast on her. She cried out, bucking her hips wildly, tearing more of her flesh. Maura was a glutton for pain and that was something he would never deny her.

CHAPTER SEVEN

Cat stared blankly at the computer screen in front of her. She refused to cry this year. She had to be strong, if not for herself, for Shane. It was the three-year anniversary of Molly's tragic death and Cat's reawakening, as Claude had deemed it. The first year had been the hardest, dealing with the loss of her best friend and her life as she knew it. Cat had given up everything to go into hiding, but how could she complain? She was living the life her best friend had so desperately wanted. One Molly had deserved to have. This year she was not going to cry. She was going to be happy, and she was going to get Shane to come out of the impossible hole of despair he seemed to have dug for himself.

"How's the site coming?" Claude asked, sitting across the table from her. They weren't exactly friends yet, but they were cordial to each other. One positive that had come from being turned was that it had given Cat the opportunity to quit her boring IT job and focus on her dream career as an independent software developer. She did almost all of her work over the internet, only meeting with a client once or twice in person.

"I'm almost finished with this one," Cat said, taking the mug of blood he handed her.

"Good, then we can work on fencing this evening," Xander said, appearing in the doorway of the kitchen.

"Seriously? Why do I need to learn to fence?" Cat asked. Xander smirked.

"To teach you discipline," he said.

She chugged the last of her breakfast.

"Discipline! I need discipline? I'm not the one who turned an innocent girl against her will. No offense Claude," Cat ranted.

By the time she had finished her rant, she was across the room directly in front of Xander with no idea how she got there. Her body always seemed to have a mind of its own when he was around. To think she had thought of him as some kind of savior when in reality, he was the bane of her existence.

"You've just proved my point," Xander's voice was low and gravelly, his face mere inches from hers.

Cat's body felt heated and not out of anger. She studied his face, the flare of his nostrils, the ever-present stubble on his chin, the way his gold-flecked eyes held a hint of passion. Cat was mesmerized for a bit but finally managed to pull her eyes away and put distance between them.

"Fine, fencing," she grumbled and stomped back over to her computer.

"Fighting already," Shane said, sitting next to Cat.

Instinctively, she leaned over, resting her head on his shoulder. Shane had shut everyone out but Cat after the accident. Over the years, he had very much become a brother to her.

"No, Xander just needed a reminder of his place," Cat said, and Shane nodded.

"Glad someone is up for the job," he said, shooting Xander a look before taking a sip of his breakfast.

Xander growled and left the room, leaving Cat, Shane, and Claude to enjoy breakfast without him.

* * *

Infuriating. That was the word to describe the petite and feisty woman that had just stood up to him. She was so very unaware that she held power over him; only one other person ever had. Xander didn't like it a single bit. Since that first night, when he'd seen her laying there lifeless, he had been enthralled.

He'd seen her beauty through the damage of the accident. Her almond-shaped eyes, full lips, and shapely hips had awakened something deep inside him. The bruises had faded quickly due to the Vampire blood coursing through her, changing her, revealing the perfect complexion of her cocoa-hued skin.

He needed to be around her, needed to care for her, and in his own way, he had. He took time out of his evenings to watch over her the few moments Shane had ever stepped away from her side that first year. He had forced himself into her daily life by insisting she needed "training." With her salty attitude, Claude had gladly relinquished his duties as sire to Xander.

The first year had been French lessons. After months of being huddled over books with her, he decided he needed something that required more space. Next came riding lessons, but the sight of her astride a horse, moving with the majestic animal, had only made his situation worse. She got under his skin, and he couldn't allow that.

* * *

"You know he means well," Shane said.

Cat sat up, looking him in the eyes, or at least trying to. Shane avoided most eye contact nowadays.

"Means well? Seriously? His lessons are brutal. I mean first with the languages, which wasn't that bad but I was bored to tears the entire time, then the horseback riding where I was so sore I could barely walk, and now with fencing. This isn't about discipline—it's about him causing me strife in any way possible on a daily basis," she said.

Claude laughed.

"I honestly don't think that's it," Claude said.

She rolled her eyes at him.

"Why, because he's upfront about it, while you pretend to be on my side?"

Claude nodded.

"If Xander had it out for you, he would have just kicked you out of the house. Especially with the way you two fight. I'm surprised he hasn't buried you in a coffin out back," Claude said, and Shane nodded in agreement.

"He's already asked me if I would be okay with it," Shane said.

Cat glared at him.

"He did what?" she growled and stormed from the kitchen, traveling up to her room to change. If he wanted a fencing partner today, he surely had one. He was going to get more than he bargained for.

***

Xander knew something was wrong when he entered the courtyard. He could feel it in the air as he exited the double doors from the library. For one, Cat was already there and warmed up. Usually, she would show up purposefully late and with an attitude. When Cat spotted him and actually smiled his way, he knew that today was not going to be the usual fencing practice.

She allowed him to warm up a bit before he began his instruction. For once, she listened to him without complaint, but the tension in her body told him that her calm demeanor was all a farce. His instincts were right; as soon as they began to pare, she attacked with a force and skill he had been unprepared for.

***

Cat was furious, and she let out all of her frustrations on him. She tried not to think about the fact that her frustration was built more on pent up sexual need than anger over his contempt for her. Nothing else seemed to matter but the attack, and soon she had him winded and disarmed on the ground, the tip of her saber pointed directly over his heart.

"You wanted to bury me in the backyard," she growled.

Of all the reactions she had expected, he had the nerve to laugh. Not his usual chuckle but a full-bellied laugh.

"It crossed my mind, yes," he said, pushing her saber away from his heart.

He stood and pulled his face shield off. Cat did the same, enjoying the fresh air on her face.

"You think it's funny? I didn't ask for this, you know," she began, but he put his hand over her mouth. She was shocked into silence.

An unwelcome jolt of awareness shot through her, flooding her body with all sorts of warm tingly feelings she had no reason to feel. It wasn't like it was the first time they had ever touched. Before it had always been accidental brushes but no real skin to skin contact—at least, not in a really long time. She knew he had felt it too, because he instantly snatched his hand away and left her standing like an idiot, alone in the courtyard.

* * *

Xander cursed himself silently as he fled the courtyard. He had just wanted to shut her up, not feel whatever it was that had overcome him when his hand had covered those full, yet venomous, lips of hers. He wondered if female vampires could actually be poisonous. He'd had his fair share of experience with the terror a female vampire could wrought. He shook his head; Cat was most certainly not like Maura. Xander rubbed his palm against his pants, trying to stop the tingling sensation left behind from the feel of Cat's lips. Maura had never elicited this response out of him, he thought as he brushed past Claude on his way to his room. He quickened his pace, heading straight for the shower. Not only was he sweaty, but he had a more obvious problem to deal with. He hoped Claude hadn't noticed the excess bulge in his fencing costume as he passed.

* * *

Claude smiled to himself as he watched Xander retreat to his room. He hadn't missed Xander's agitated and aroused state. Fencing hadn't been that stimulating when Claude had learned. With those two circling each other the past few years, being stuck in the house had become a lot more entertaining. He wondered what state Cat would be in if Xander was in such a huff. Claude headed to the courtyard to find out.

It took Cat a moment to regain her wits, but when she did, she was even more upset than before, not only with Xander but with herself.

"This is fascinating," Claude said, breaking into Cat's musings.

"What is?" Cat asked, focusing on him.

"I think I've figured out the hostility between you and Xander," he said.

He winked at her before leaving her alone once again. Cat just rolled her eyes and headed to her room to take a shower. She suddenly felt extremely tired and achy.

* * *

Xander was exactly where Claude had expected him to be. It was all Claude could do to keep a straight face as he made his presence known. Xander was such a serious man; he always had been. It gave Claude great joy to tease him when his feathers were already ruffled.

"As her sire, I give you my permission to—well, I won't embarrass you, but I wish you both all the happiness in the world," Claude said with a smirk on his face.

"I'm sure knocking before you enter was in fashion even in your day," Xander replied, not looking up from his desk.

"You wouldn't have answered, and then I wouldn't have gotten to see the relief on your face," Claude chided, then turned, leaving Xander alone with his musings.

Claude seriously hoped Xander would give in to his obvious infatuation with Cat. Other than Shane, the only obstacle was Cat herself, and well—Cat was quite an obstacle. As soon as he met Cat that terrible night, he had known that Xander had been a lot more suited for her. Shane might have lost his heart that night, but it seemed he had given Xander back his.

Cat wrapped the blanket tighter around herself. After the shower, she started getting chills and a major headache, so she just crawled into bed. She hadn't been aware that she could get sick as a Vampire. That wasn't mentioned in any of the lore she had combed through during her second year of Vampire life.

Maybe her breakfast had been a little old, but then wouldn't the others be sick as well? It could be possible, considering she had taken Xander down a lot easier than she had expected. Maybe it was the stress of the day that had her out of sorts. Maybe it would all go away after a little sleep. Cat curled tighter into herself and closed her eyes. She would get a little extra sleep.

"Catherine, help me, please," a voice said, startling Cat awake. It sounded so much like Molly! She searched the dark room but could see nothing.

"Help me! I'm alive, Catherine; I'm alive," the voice said again.

Cat felt like she was wading through ice water as she walked cautiously through the dark room. The voice had definitely been Molly, but she had never used Cat's full name when she was alive. In fact, Molly had been the only person to call her Cat in the beginning.

"Where are you?" Cat called out, but the only reply she received was another cry for help.

"Molly, please! I need you to tell me how to get to you. It's dark. I can't see you," Cat cried, frantic to find her friend.

"I'm right here," Molly said.

The voice was directly behind her. Cat turned around, throwing her arms around the petite body that was so familiar, only for her skin to begin tingling. It was barely noticeable at first but quickly became uncomfortable, reminding Cat of a chemical burn she had gotten from her first home relaxer.

"You left me to burn, and now so will you all!" Molly growled. Her voice held a demonic edge to it now.

Cat took a step back and really looked at what was in front of her. Molly's face was twisted with rage, and flames sprouted up all around her. Molly seemed unfazed by the flames, but Cat felt it all; she felt it everywhere. She saw her skin on fire, the flesh falling away in charred layers. Cat screamed as not only physical but emotional pain ripped through her, but even her screams couldn't drown out Molly's maniacal laughter.

CHAPTER EIGHT

"Cat, wake up!" Xander said, frantic as he held an ice rag to her forehead.

He had come to her room to apologize for asking Shane if he could bury her. Xander had knocked several times before he heard her whimpering. Normally, he would have left her alone. It was not his to console, yet, he hadn't been able to control his urge to make sure she was alright. Xander had been sure he would find her watching some sad movie, but instead, she had been unconscious, writhing in pain with some sort of fever. The ice rag he had gotten wasn't helping to cool her fast enough. In fact, almost as soon as he had placed the rag on her burning skin, it had begun to steam itself.

He had to do something fast, or Cat may be lost forever. He had seen the way fevers could kill or at the very least strip a person of their faculties. He ripped the covers away from her body. He took a step back as he noticed she was completely naked except for a necklace he had thought he would never see again.

Xander almost forgot the peril Cat was in as old memories flooded his mind. Memories of Rachel, the woman he had loved and lost so long ago. Maura had demanded Rachel as the first victim Xander would bring to her. Xander hadn't known what would happen to Rachel; he'd been too lost in everything that was Maura. He remembered how Rachel had begged and pleaded with him for help. How he had been unable to do anything as Maura held him at bay.

"You belong to me alone," Maura had said before sinking her fangs into Rachel's delicate shoulder. She had only released him after Rachel had been completely drained. It was only for a brief moment that he had been allowed to feel, and all that he felt was an overwhelming loss not only for Rachel but for his own humanity. He had rushed to Rachel's side, holding her lifeless body against his. It was the last time he had ever shown signs of weakness in front of Maura.

He'd buried Rachel in the customs of her people, burning her body on a pyre, but he had removed her necklace. She had told him it was a family heirloom, so he had made sure to return it to her family in the dark of the night. Attached had been a letter warning them of the danger Maura presented to the rest of the young woman in the family. He had been glad when they had left the village a few days later. Xander shook off his shock and picked up Cat, holding her tightly as she continued to thrash wildly against him. He carried her to the bathroom, where he placed her in the tub and began to fill it with cold water.

***

Cat woke up gasping for air a few minutes later. She struggled with an imaginary Molly demon until she realized the arms encircling her weren't constricting her like in her dream. She was no longer on fire—instead, she was freezing in an ice bath with Xander staring down at her. Concern showed clearly on his face as he held her in the water.

Cat was so relieved; she threw her arms around him and

began to sob. Xander held her, stroking her back until she calmed down. It was only then that Cat realized she was completely naked and clinging to Xander of all people. Cat jerked away and glared at him. Xander had the nerve to blush and look away. Cat folded her arms across her ample bosom and curled her legs up in a futile attempt at modesty.

"What are you doing in my room?" Cat asked.

Xander stood, turning completely away as he began to leave the room. Cat jumped up from the tub, but her legs gave out, tipping her over the edge. Before Cat knew it, she was back in Xander's arms, her naked body flush against his, water soaking through his clothes. The warmth of him felt so amazing after the cold of the ice bath she had just been in. Her breath caught as their eyes met. Cat began to feel warm and tingly for a completely different reason.

* * *

Xander knew that he should pull away, but the way she was looking up at him, so innocently as she pressed her seductress body against his, wouldn't allow him. His lips were touching hers before his brain could catch up. He would have pulled away if she had fought him—if she made any move to let him know she didn't want him. She didn't, so Xander deepened the kiss, coaxing her mouth open with his tongue.

Xander was completely unprepared for the sweet honeysuckle taste of her mouth. It was intoxicating in its purity. He nearly lost control. In that moment of recklessness, the urge to see if her blood was just as potent had him struggling with the monster inside of him. He fought to maintain his carefully crafted façade of humanity; it was all he had left. Cat moaned and reached up to grab his hair. She pulled Xander closer, changing the angle of the kiss. Changing the momentum startled Xander's beast into submission and allowed him to enjoy the moment as the man he wished he could be again.

* * *

Cat was so going to hate herself for this later, but after the dream she just had and five years of celibacy—she fully intended on enjoying everything Xander had to offer her. As soon as his lips had touched hers, Cat felt herself melting at her core. She was more than ready for Xander to take her. She needed him in a way she had never needed a man. Then again, Xander wasn't exactly a man, although the large erection he was sporting in his linen pants was evidence of his manhood in itself. Without breaking the kiss, Cat wedged enough space between them to work for her hands down to his pants. He was driving her insane with lust, and his clothing was the only thing between her and the instrument of her desire. She began to undress him, but his hands came over hers, stopping her manic fumbling.

* * *

Xander felt Cat's slim fingers toying with his belt, and he knew he had to stop her if only for a minute. As much as he wanted her, he would take her the correct way. This might be nothing more than a fling to her, but for him, it needed to be more. He needed to have her on his terms and for her to realize that this was more to him than giving in to hormones. Xander moved her hands away and scooped her up into his arms, breaking their kiss just long enough to carry her from the bathroom and back to the bed.

He wasted no time; after laying her on the bed, he moved away from her just as long as it took for him to strip off his own clothing. Cat reached for him as soon as he was naked, and he didn't deny her. He fell upon her, showering her with kisses, exploring her body with his plate-sized hands. Cat hated to admit how often she had dreamed of this, of feeling his roughened palms running over her heated skin. Skimming the edge of her breasts, lightly chaffing her already over-sensitized nipples, his hands massaged and kneaded her flesh until she was a quivering, cooing ball of arousal.

She was so soft and feminine under his rough hands. Xander was almost afraid of how fragile she seemed beneath him. Cat writhed, urging him to touch her lower, but he didn't give in. As much as he wanted to touch her there, he needed to take his time. He kept his hands moving, skirting the area she so desperately wanted him to touch. It seemed he could never get enough of the feel of her.

The contrast of her normally abrasive personality and the way she begged him now had Xander wanting to give her anything and everything she wanted. Her eyes were so full of delicious promise that his body nearly exploded on it alone. He was so aroused at this point, it was painful, and he had no choice but to finally give them both what they so desperately wanted, and so he did. Xander kissed her possessively as his hands traveled to previously unknown territory. He groaned as he felt just how truly ready she was for him. His fingers traced the edges of her slick folds before he let them dip tentatively into her hot wet cave.

Cat arched into him as he pressed two fingers past her slick folds and into her dripping wet core. Her body's response to this minor penetration made her realize just how long it had truly been for her. She was so soft and pliant under his rough, strong hands. The contrast only intensified his need to be inside her, but he promised himself that he would take things slow. He would make sure that she was completely sated by night's end, and then they would have a serious talk.

* * *

Cat couldn't form any complete thought as pleasure began to build between her legs. She had almost no control over her body as it moved on its own, pressing her core closer to Xander's hands and her chest closer to his mouth as he teased her with feather light kisses just shy of the places she really wanted to feel his lips. Cat groaned with frustration as he evaded her nipple once again, and in response, he increased the pressure of his thumb against her clit, sending her over the edge. Cat cried out as waves of pleasure ripped through her, prolonged by Xander's steady, controlled movement.

* * *

Xander fought back his own groan as her muscles began to spasm around his fingers. She had no idea how close he was to losing control at the sight of her in the throes of passion. She was beautiful and wild and all his. He brought his fingers up to taste her. She was ambrosia, and he wanted more of her.

He moved down her body quickly, placing his tongue where his fingers had just been. He licked her, plunging his tongue into her core, making love to her with his mouth the way he intended to with other parts of him later. He suckled her clit, reveling in the feel of her body pulsing in desire and enjoying the look of surprise on her face as he savored her. When he felt her orgasm start to build again, he slid up her body, kissing her on her face and neck while positioning his throbbing manhood at her dripping entrance.

"Mine," he growled, sliding into her torturously slow.

Xander felt like he was sliding into heaven with each inch he managed to get inside of her. She was so tight that even with ample preparation, he was hesitant to claim her the way his body and beast demanded. Instead, he gritted his teeth and took his time.

* * *

Cat chose to ignore Xander's possessive declaration as he stretched and filled her to completion. Her body was in brand new territory. It wasn't like Cat was a virgin, but this definitely felt like her first time. Her body was so tight it was almost painful the way her nerves began to shoot sparks of pleasure with every inch he moved inside of her.

It was blissful and excruciating, and, in all honesty, Cat was impatient for release. When Xander paused in his invasion of her, she wrapped her legs around his hips and pulled him in deeper. She wanted—no needed—all of him. They stayed like that for a few moments, just absorbing the feel of each other. Cat felt a stirring in her heart that she was completely unprepared for, so she tore her gaze away from his and bucked her hips against him.

Xander refused to move, pressing his hips into her, pinning her to the bed. He placed a finger under her chin, bringing her face and eyes back to him. He kissed her, holding her gaze as he rotated his hips, grinding against her. The full contact of his pelvic bone against her clit and the tip of him rubbing the furthest reaches of her core had Cat shuttering with euphoria as he continued this slow, grinding pace.

"Xander, please," she cried, trying to speed up the pace, but he wasn't budging. He was in control of this, and he would speed up when he wanted, and only if he wanted to. That knowledge made Cat hotter than in her dream but in a good way. Cat had never known she could get off on being possessed so completely.

* * *

Xander watched the various emotions flashing across Cat's face as they made love. She was so beautiful and full of life, and he loved her. Xander's heart skipped a beat as the realization hit him. Maybe it was just seeing the necklace that had reawakened something inside of him he thought was gone, but from the beginning, Cat had meant something to him. He hadn't been able to stay away from her, and now that he had her completely, there was no way he was ever letting her go. He just had to get her on the same page.

* * *

The next night, Cat awoke trapped under Xander's heavy arm. She smiled to herself as she remembered last night and how he had brought her to climax over and over again before allowing himself his own release. She had never been with a more selfless lover, but then again, everything about last night had been new. After the first time, Cat had enjoyed showing him just how adventurous and flexible she was in bed, and she hoped maybe they could trade their fencing lessons for more carnal activities in the future.

She shifted a little, trying to get free from his massive arm, and ended up having to slide out of his grip as if it were a tunnel. It wasn't until she was free of him that she felt the weight of something heavy around her neck. She tensed and looked down to see a strange stone pendant hanging from a dark metal chain around her neck. It was surprisingly delicate-looking for the amount of weight it carried.

Had Xander given her this gift sometime during the night? Cat was confused as she looked at the necklace in the mirror, at least until she looked up and saw the evil visage of Molly in the mirror instead of her own reflection. The necklace on Molly's neck instead of hers. Fear raced through her veins, chilling her to the bone.

Am I still dreaming?

Cat closed her eyes, biting back a scream as pain ripped through her once again. As quickly as it began, the pain ceased. Cat cautiously opened her eyes to find the mirror back to normal, but the necklace was still around her neck.

What the hell is going on?

CHAPTER NINE

Molly woke up from her dream, angry and alone once again. She hadn't believed a word Declan said when she had woken up the first time. She had believed that Shane would never have left her to die, and neither would Cat. Only after three years without so much as a word from either of them, she finally faced the facts. Shane had lied to her and left her for dead, and her best friend couldn't have cared less. If Declan hadn't been there then, she wouldn't be alive right now. If that night had taught her anything, it was to be careful what you wished for.

Despite being betrayed and lonely, there were a few positives to the outcome of that night. She had finally learned to stop being so naïve, she was still alive, and she was living in Scotland. Molly had always wanted to travel, and now she was living abroad. Declan had promised her once they wrapped up the excavation that he would make sure she was able to travel more, but for now, she spent her days assisting his girlfriend, Maura, at the estate.

Molly's face twisted with disgust as loud moans came through the thin walls of the apartment she shared with Declan. Apparently, Maura had decided to stay over. She usually stayed at the estate where Declan worked, but more recently, she had been staying at the apartment more often. Molly wasn't a huge fan of Maura, but she owed her everything. It was Maura who had given her purpose in this new life. Molly hadn't been the first woman to be betrayed by Shane, but she would be sure that she was the last.

If only Cat hadn't betrayed her as well. Molly touched her neck, reaching for the necklace that had given her the power to reach out to Cat but froze when she realized it wasn't there. She panicked, searching her entire room, but it was nowhere to be found. This was not good. Molly had to find it before Maura asked for it back.

* * *

Shane paced angrily across the study as Claude watched, amused. Who knew that today would be so entertaining? First, with Xander and Cat's attraction finally being acknowledged and now Shane showing any kind of emotion after the accident three years ago.

"Seriously, dude, this isn't a bad thing," Claude said, but Shane just continued pacing.

"Not bad? Not bad! He was against me turning Molly, furious that Cat was mixed up in all of this, and now he's taking advantage of her," he growled.

Claude could only shake his head. He had expected Shane to be upset, but this outrage was completely over the top. Xander hadn't been against him turning Molly, at least not after meeting her, and of course, Xander would be upset about Cat. Xander hated when things didn't go according to plan. On top of that, Cat was absolutely infuriating to be around. Probably more so for Xander since he had wanted her since the first day she set foot in the house.

"I gave him my permission; besides, they have been circling

the bedroom since the first day she woke up. You were too upset to see it, but Xander has been fighting this attraction to her since the beginning, and you want to know why?" Claude asked, and Shane paused to glare at him.

"Because he wanted to wait until she was well enough," he said.

Claude sighed.

"No, because he knew that you both needed time. Whatever happened to get them both to give in must have been something big. I'm just glad that it won't be like a crowded sauna every time those two are in the same room," Claude said, standing.

He left the room shaking his head as Shane continued to pace. Claude hoped that the old Shane would find a way back, and soon. This new Shane was a little too quirky for Claude's liking. It almost reminded him of the strung-out behavior he'd seen in Shane's past research.

CHAPTER TEN

Xander rolled over to find he was alone in bed. He jerked up and scrambled out of bed, searching the room for Cat. His heart began to race until he noticed the light on in the bathroom. He sighed with relief before lazily getting up and meandering over to the door. He knocked softly, hoping she wouldn't try to shut him out so soon. What they had shared was more than Xander could have imagined or hoped for. There was no way she could deny the chemistry between them now nor would Xander let her.

Cat opened the door looking tired and pale, completely devoid of the glow of a woman who had been well-loved the entire night before. Xander's smile faltered, and he pulled her into his arms. She looked awful, and Xander cursed himself for rushing things with her. She had been so sick the night before, and he felt like a total ass for not putting her wellbeing before his own urges, regardless of how much she seemed to enjoy last night's activity.

* * *

Cat was completely unprepared for Xander comforting her. She had opened the door to tell him that although last night had been amazing, it didn't change things about their relationship. She should have known better. As soon as she opened the door and saw the love in his eye, however, reflecting the same commitment she had seen in his gaze all last night, she knew he would be much harder to shake. Now in the early evening, they stood facing each other, embracing each other even as they envisioned different realities.

He was probably thinking of a future with her, while all she could think about was the crazy dream that had started it all. Cat had been shaken by the discovery of the necklace, but it was the discovery that she couldn't take it off that had her worried. The appearance of the necklace meant last night hadn't just been a dream; it had been real. Cat hated to think about what that meant. Molly was dead—she had gone to the funeral. She had seen Molly's severed head, as much as she tried to get that image of her friend out of her mind.

"Will you tell me what's wrong?" Xander asked.

She finally pulled away from him. Cat just shook her head and kissed him. He wanted to pull away and get answers from her, but what she needed now was comforting. Xander would get her to talk later, but for now, he would do anything to make her feel better, and they both knew exactly how to achieve that.

Cat pulled Xander into the bathroom and shut the door behind her. She knew he wanted to talk; she could see it in those expressive hazel eyes of his. It was unnerving how open and easy to read he was to her now. She shook those thoughts from her head as she dragged him into the warm spray of the shower. After an intimate shower, they lay cuddled in bed, and Xander decided to share with her his story.

"I was twenty-five when I fell into Maura's web. I had been out drinking with friends, and she caught my eye. I didn't approach her, though; I was already in love with Rachel. I had grown up with Rachel, and she was a lovely, sweet girl. I had intended to marry her. My friends and I got into an argument with one of the men at the bar. The man was so belligerent I had to call him out. If I had known it was set up, I would never have followed him out behind the alehouse. He had far superior strength, and he wounded me severely. I only remember being cold and alone on the ground and then waking up tied to Maura's bed. She forced me to pleasure her, even after I told her about Rachel.

Maura told me I belonged to her and that I could only stay with Rachel if I brought her to Maura, let her turn her. I was so drunk with the power being a Vampire afforded me that I believed her, so that night, I went to Rachel. She had been so worried about me since no one had seen me for weeks. She didn't question when I asked her to run away with me. I promised her the world. I promised her my love. I promised her that we would be together forever, but it was all a lie. As soon as Rachel was in Maura's clutches, Maura drained her dry, and I was powerless to stop her. Maura not only took my heart from me that day, she tainted it somehow. After that night, I was jaded and a puppet. As much as I hated Maura, I obeyed her every wish.

It was a long time before I was able to break her hold on me and on the others. It took a lot from me, and I made sure I took everything from her before I left her rotted corpse buried beneath her hell gate," Xander said.

Cat snuggled into him more.

She could practically feel his pain as he told her the story, and she felt herself tearing in grief for what he had gone through. Cat felt compelled to share with him her dream now, and so she began.

"I saw Molly, but it wasn't Molly; it was someone else. It was something else, and it wanted me to be scared. It wanted me to feel pain, and so it burned me alive. I could feel the flames as if they were real. I could smell my own burning flesh, and Molly just stood there with satisfaction on her face as I burned to death before her eyes. I think Molly is alive," she said, and Xander frowned.

"That's impossible. If there had been any way, Shane would have turned her," Xander said.

Cat nodded.

"I thought so too, but after this dream, I just know. In the dream, she was wearing this necklace. Now I have it, and I can't take it off," she said, touching the chain around her neck.

Xander sat up and tried to open the clasp of the chain. It wouldn't budge. He tried to yank it apart, but it was no use.

"This can't be. The necklace you are wearing belonged to Rachel. I returned it to her family after her death. There is no way you or Molly should have been able to come across it," he said.

The look of confusion in his eyes scared Cat more than anything. Being the oldest, Xander usually had all the answers, but this was obviously something new to him. He got out of bed and went to the door.

"Get dressed and meet me in the study in an hour," he said before leaving the room.

* * *

Xander went to the nearest phone and dialed Felix's number. Felix had been the closest to Maura out of all of them. Maybe he could offer some insight. When he didn't answer, Xander tried his office and his house phone. When he received no answer there either, Xander called the school Felix occasionally taught classes for. Felix had gone missing right before the discovery of the room below MacDonald Estate. Xander thanked the person on the other end and hung up.

This was not good. It couldn't be a mere coincidence that Felix was missing, and Cat had these creepy nightmares. He kicked himself for being so preoccupied with Cat that he had neglected to follow up with Felix sooner. Hell, even Shane who monitored the news had been too despondent over his girlfriend to keep up with the media. This was all Xander's fault. He was usually the most responsible one. He shouldn't have allowed for such an oversight. He shouldn't have allowed himself or the others to be so distracted by a mere woman.

To make matters worse, this seemed directly tied to his past. Rachel's necklace should have been lost to time along with her family. Xander should be the only person alive with knowledge of that necklace, and yet, Molly had somehow had it in her possession. Molly had used it to torment Cat with it in a dream, and now it was stuck on Cat's neck. Was this some warning from the spirit realm? Something was definitely wrong, and as much as Xander hated to acknowledge it, he would have to go to Scotland to figure out what was going on.

CHAPTER ELEVEN

"What do you mean Felix is missing? Doesn't he write at least once a year? Shouldn't you know where he is?" Claude asked, obviously upset.

Cat just sat confused as Shane, Claude and Xander talked about people and places she had never heard of before today.

"He's missing, and Maura's tomb has been found. I don't think this is a coincidence." Shane said.

Shane was grimaced at his laptop screen which was showing an article from Archaeology Daily.

Xander buried his face in his hands and Claude continued to pace around the room.

"Maybe he is moving the corpse. You know we always had the plan of burying her in the Amazon. He could just be out of reach for a while," Claude said optimistically, but Shane and Xander's expressions remained grim.

"Felix would have contacted us if he had been forced to move her. I should have realized I hadn't received any update, but I've been so caught up with everything that has happened since the accident," Xander said.

Claude flopped down on the couch next to Cat. They all made a conscious effort not to look in her direction, but Cat got the picture. Xander's statement was vague but she knew what he really meant. Cat was the distraction. He blamed this on her and it appeared so did the others.

"What made you decide to check up on him anyway? It's still a year before the next rotation," Claude said.

Xander shot him a look.

"Cat, would you mind sharing your dream with the others?" Xander said.

Cat looked tentatively at Shane.

"What?" Shane asked, and Cat looked away.

She couldn't look him in the eye and tell him Molly was still alive. After all of this time, after all the grief, she didn't want to see what her story would do to him. Cat took a deep breath and began to explain. Her foot bounced nervously as Shane just stood staring out the window. He hadn't moved or said a single word as she relayed her story.

She knew she wasn't the only one nervous about his reaction. Molly had meant so much to Shane, and now to know there was a possibility she had survived and was out there somewhere? A million and one things must be running through his mind. Claude moved to the bar and poured four tumblers of brandy. He handed everyone a glass before shooting his back and pouring another one.

Xander sat next to Cat, his arm draped protectively over her shoulder. She leaned into him, drawing on his strength as she sipped the alcohol. Even after three years, the brandy still burned her throat, while the others seemed to drink it like water.

"I'll go to Scotland and take over guarding the estate," Claude said, but Shane shook his head.

"I am next in the rotation; I'll go and report back with anything I find," he said, taking them all off guard. Claude's eyes narrowed as he took another shot.

"You have to look for Molly, and Xander has Cat now. I'll go and man the fort while you two handle your futures," Claude countered, but this time Xander shook his head.

"It's too dangerous for any one of us to go alone. All of us will go to Scotland," he said, and despite looks of protest, both Claude and Shane nodded.

"I guess I better set everything up for Cat to be by herself here," Shane said, and Cat jumped up from where she was sitting.

"What? I'm going with you!" she said, but as she looked around the room, she sank back down in defeat. This mission was definitely about their past, and as much as she knew about it, Cat was very much aware that there was a lot she still wasn't privy to.

"It's too dangerous for you to go. We have no idea what we will be walking into," Xander said, nuzzling her neck. As upset as she was, she couldn't argue with that fact. Cat silently cursed herself for not taking Xander's lessons seriously. Maybe if she had, she would be able to go with them. Sensing that the discussion was about to get serious about things they didn't want her to know, Cat excused herself and went back up to her room.

* * *

Cat hated to be excluded. Especially when this was the most excitement that had happened in the house since—well—last night. Maybe if she had actually talked to Xander instead of jumping his bones, she would have known more and been included in whatever plans the boys were making downstairs. Instead, here she was, cleaning up the mess she had made with Xander in their carnal adventures just before her complete meltdown over the necklace.

"Are you okay?" Xander asked, leaning against the side of the doorway. Cat turned to him and smiled. She had hoped he would come to her after he was done talking with the others.

"I'm fine; it just got a little too hot in here," she said, and he laughed. He crossed the room and sat next to her on the bed.

"Yeah, I know what you mean," he said, smiling seductively at her.

They sat in silence for a few seconds before he started caressing her arm. Cat moved off the bed and away from him. She had decided she wanted to talk, not get swept up in him again. It had been far too long since she'd been intimate with someone, and she didn't trust that she could stop herself. She didn't trust that Xander would allow her to stop.

Sensing her withdrawal, Xander followed her across the room. He knew she wanted to talk about what was going on, but he had other ideas. Funny how the tables had turned in just a few hours. He looked into her eyes, and it was like a moth drawn to the flame. Their bodies came together and then their lips. She wrapped her arms around his neck, and his hands rested on her hips before he became bolder and palmed both cheeks of her round bottom. He groped her, pulling her harder against him as they kissed.

Cat's body was aflame once again, this time in a good way, as his rough palms skimmed the bare flesh of her belly and up further to cup and fondle her breast. She moaned into his mouth as he began to play with her nipple. Her body began to rub against his involuntarily as if it had a mind of its own.

Cat struggled to maintain control. She wanted Xander, had wanted him for a long time, and now that she had him, he was leaving, possibly never to return. She needed this to be good, and for that, she needed to keep some control over the situation and her body.

In one swift movement, he was gone from her mouth, and they were on the bed once again. His mouth was on her, suckling and nipping. His hand moved between her legs again. He rubbed her clit until her head fell back, and she moaned out to the open air. Xander needed her just as desperately as she needed him, but he was trying to take things slow. He wanted her to feel how much he cared for her because as much as Xander hated to admit it, tonight could very well be one of their last.

For the next three days, while Xander and Shane handled the travel arrangements, Claude gave Cat a crash course in the logistics of being a Vampire in the modern world. She met with the blood supplier and had to memorize countless passwords and secret handshakes. By the end of the three days, Cat wondered what the hell she had been doing the past few years because learning to be self-sufficient sure as hell wasn't one of them.

She had obviously taken a lot for granted, and as much as she had wished for freedom from the mansion before, Cat was now aware that she had been very far from that goal. If things hadn't turned out the way they had, Cat was completely unsure how she would ever survive being alone as a Vampire without the help of Xander, Claude, and Shane.

It also begged the question of how Molly had managed it. Not only would she have had to have been brought back, but she would have needed to learn how to survive the major adjustment that was life as a Vampire. Where had she stayed during the day? How did she get the blood she needed without running into serious complications like hiding bodies? Unless she had already made connections to get bagged blood. Cat didn't even want to think of what it was like to feed on a live person.

Although she felt the urge to bite Xander multiple times, especially during sex, the part of her that was still human had a hard time reconciling that new part of her existence. Maybe there would be a time to explore that drinking option later, as long as the boys came back alive and well and hopefully with good news.

"Be safe," Cat called out to the guys as they headed out the door.

She was beginning to miss them already, and she hoped they all came back safely. In the meantime, she had plenty to keep her occupied but a whole lot of nothing to keep her entertained. The mansion now felt like a giant empty space instead of the home it had become for her. At least now she could finally do some snooping in Xander's quarters. He shouldn't mind now that they were intimate. She was curious to see how he lived.

CHAPTER TWELVE

"This place still gives me the creeps," Shane said with a visible shiver. Claude just looked over at him and shrugged.

"It's an old building; that's all," he said, but the slight waver in his voice gave a clue that he was just as shaken by being back there.

Xander studied MacDonald estate looking for any signs that would alert them of trouble, but he saw nothing. Everything seemed to be precisely the same as the pictures Felix had routinely sent. Well, everything except the number of people now milling around the grounds.

The house was the same, overwhelming and pretentious in its stone design. It stood like a fortress, in the center of everything. The grounds surrounding it were still just as manicured as always, and the woods at the back edge of the property was just as ominous as ever, especially since it shielded the drop-off point of a very steep cliff edge. The cliff was the only area not surrounded by a massive stone wall, for obvious reasons.

With the discovery of the cavern beneath the herb garden, there was more interest in possible sites elsewhere on the grounds. Also, with Felix gone, they made much more headway than any of them would have liked but with no news of any remains discovered. Xander wasn't sure whether that was a good thing or not.

Xander wasn't happy to be back here at this godforsaken

fortress either, but over the past three days, they had exhausted all other possibilities. If there had been no foul play, this was the only place left for there to be any clue as to what happened with Felix. If only they had listened to Shane and sealed the tomb in with concrete instead of dirt and gravel! They would never have needed to keep such a vigilant guard, and there wouldn't have been any discoveries at all.

Xander shook his head to clear his thoughts. Now was not the time to dwell on what could have and should have been done. They needed to find out what happened to Felix. The faster they figured things out, the sooner he could get back to Cat. Xander shuddered to think what too much time alone would do to her newfound cordiality.

* * *

Declan looked down at the three men standing at the edges of the estate, and his senses went on immediate red alert. This couldn't possibly be good. It was definitely too early in the plan for them to be showing up now. He stepped away from the window and turned to see Maura smiling.

"What did you do?" Declan said, careful not to sound upset. The last thing he needed on top of everything else was to piss off Maura. He had learned that on day one, when they destroyed Felix Aiken.

Maura may have let Declan take the last of his blood, but what Maura had done to what remained of him was something Declan could only describe as total obliteration. The only good thing about it was that it made for easy cleanup. There wasn't a piece big enough for Declan to even bother trying to hide. Felix was still scattered around what was supposed to be Maura's tomb, and if Maura had her way, the three men on the front lawn would be scattered there as well.

* * *

"Did they bring the girl?" Maura asked, choosing to ignore Declan's little fit of temper. He didn't need to understand what was happening. He just needed to obey her orders. Sure, Maura hadn't even expected them to come so soon, but it didn't matter to her either way. They had come, and they would not only die for betraying her, but they would suffer too.

"No. It's just the three," Declan said, and Maura frowned.

"Well, that just won't do. Bring Molly to me," Maura said, and Declan nodded before disappearing from the room.

When he returned with Molly a short time later, she looked panic-stricken, which made Maura smile. Declan knew Maura enjoyed pain and discomfort in a way that bordered on mental illness. It was one of the things that kept him around.

"Declan, leave us," Maura said.

He looked ready to protest but did as she asked anyway.

Maura would definitely have to watch him. He was still so willful, even after she had enthralled him. The last person she allowed to be so had been Xander, and that almost got her killed. She turned her attention back to Molly.

"Did you do it?" she demanded, and Molly nodded, but Maura still wasn't convinced.

"And the necklace?" Maura asked.

Molly jerked, her eyes skittering around the room, anxious to be anywhere but on Maura. Maura fought the urge to get up and snap the little twit's neck. This was why Maura was not in the business of turning women. They were too much drama for so little use. Men were much easier to control. They were ruled by their dicks and easily led by them. Women were much more valuable for consumption.

Building her strength and her beauty often required a complete sacrifice of body and soul from her female victims. Molly, however, was neither young enough or beautiful enough for that purpose. Frankly, her usefulness spawned merely from her attachment to her ex-slave, Shane. Which meant as tired as Maura was of dealing with the woman, Molly was more useful to her alive.

"The necklace?" Maura repeated, willing Molly. This was the first time Maura had used any controlling power on Molly, and the fear in her eyes piqued Maura's curiosity.

"It's gone," Molly stammered, and Maura's lips thinned with anger.

* * *

"What do you mean gone?" she screeched, and Molly gasped as she realized for the first time that Maura's eyes were soulless black pits.

"When I woke up, it wasn't there. I searched my entire room, but I couldn't find it," Molly rushed to get out.

With each word, she felt as if fingers were curling tighter around her neck, choking her. Maura looked extremely angry, and it was all Molly could do to keep herself from running out of the room when Maura finally dismissed her. It wasn't until Molly was safely back in her office that she finally took a clear breath.

***

"Let's take a look," Xander said, taking off towards the entrance of the estate before the others could complain.

Before Xander could put the finger on the door, it swung open, revealing a stocky young man in his mid-twenties to early thirties, if Xander had to guess. The young man smiled pleasantly, but it didn't reach his eyes. This man was definitely on edge and definitely not human. Xander returned the smile and pushed his way in. The lack of resistance in the man told Xander that he was a fairly new Vampire.

"Hello, my name is Declan. I am in charge of the dig. Are you here to see the latest progress?" the man asked.

Xander just nodded, studying the man further. There were still plenty of humans on the grounds, and from what he could tell, Declan wouldn't risk trying anything, at least not right now. Xander allowed him to give him a tour of the interior of the house, pretending that he was just like any other person interested in the new discoveries, but all the while, he kept watch for any signs of foul play. Hopefully, Claude and Shane weren't letting the past shake them too much and were doing as thorough of a job as Xander was.

* * *

Cat woke with a start, her hand clutching the necklace she still wasn't able to take off. It had only been a few days since the others had left, but she never felt so alone in her life. It only made matters worse that she kept having nightmares, all of them involving the torture of the men she had come to think of as family.

It sucked that it had taken her this long to realize how

much they all meant to her. Even Claude seemed like a brother to her, and Xander—well—she preferred not to think of the new emotions she felt for him. She prayed they would all come back soon and with good news.

Giving up on sleep, Cat made her way down to the kitchen. Maybe pretending to eat some chocolate ice cream would end her worrying. Cat was really not enjoying losing her taste. Even the sourest and spiciest of things were beginning to taste like paste. Blood had started to taste better, however, which as her new diet staple, wasn't a big positive, but a positive nonetheless. With the guys absent, Cat just grabbed a spoon and the carton out of the fridge. With snack in hand, she made her way back down the empty hallway to Shane's den. It was set up like the ultimate man cave, with movie theater-style recliners and a white wall ideal for the use of a projector.

Cat was just about to sink into the supple leather seating when she felt something cold brush against her neck. She stiffened and turned, only to find nothing. The house wasn't particularly the drafty sort, but with the dreams Cat had been having lately, she chalked it up to simple home alone jitters. At least until she heard the soft laughter coming from behind her.

Cat jumped up from her seat, completely disregarding her snack as she came face to face with a ghost. At least she hoped it was a ghost, or better yet, just a figment of her imagination. She could totally see cabin fever being a real thing.

"Don't be afraid. I'm here to help," the ghostly figure said in a feminine voice.

"I don't need any help," Cat said, deciding that she was probably still dreaming.

"But you do. You and everyone you care about are in great danger," the figure said.

Suddenly, the projector turned on, and images began to flash on the wall behind Cat. She cautiously turned, taking a few steps back so she could see what was being shown on the wall, as well as keeping an eye on her unwelcome guest. The images were flashing too fast for Cat to really see anything, but she recognized the faces of Claude and Xander in some of them. Then everything went still, and one image held. It was a woman dressed in a flowing red gown; her red painted lips curved into a menacing grin that flashed her fangs. Something deep within told Cat that this woman was Maura.

"The necklace you're wearing was once worn by an innocent young girl. This monster stole it from a grave to use against Xander. She cursed it with the last of her dark magic, the same magic she used to control Xander and the others for so long. By wearing the necklace, you control this power now," the figure said, and, as if in agreement, the stone pendant began to feel heated against Cat's skin.

"Great, just what I always wanted. An ancient cursed accessory that apparently goes with everything," Cat quipped.

The ghostly figure moved closer to Cat until she was shivering from the cold that seemed to emanate from it and sink into her very soul.

"Don't take this lightly. My soul is cursed because of it, and if you don't take heed of this warning, your soul will be cursed as well. Maura will come for her power, and you will have to be strong enough to keep it from her. I believe you are, which is why I made sure the necklace came to you. Don't make me regret that decision. Protect the necklace and protect Xander," the figure said.

Then as quickly as it had appeared, it was gone. The air in the room quickly returned to a normal temperature, and Cat couldn't help the way her body felt drained of all energy. She flopped back down in the leather chair and drifted off into a tormented sleep.

CHAPTER THIRTEEN

Claude forced his arms to his sides as he made his way through the densely wooded area along the edge of the MacDonald Estate. After the long plane ride to Scotland, this jaunt wasn't exactly where he would like to be. Still, it was important they figure out what exactly had happened here. Where had Felix disappeared to? Had he met an untimely end as they all thought? The flight had given them plenty of time to speculate but now they were after the facts. Claude held little hope of finding Felix alive. If something had happened that forced Felix into hiding, he would have contacted them or at least left some sort of trail for them to follow.

That was Claude's task now, to see if Felix had left a clue at the predetermined spot. They had agreed long ago that they would leave some kind of message in the hollow trunk of a tree that sat in the middle of a clearing. Shane knew the wooded area better than Claude, but Shane was less himself now than he had ever been since the loss of Molly. So, Claude had let Shane take the easier task of mingling amongst the workers, trying to gather information from them. Any rumors as to the whereabouts of Felix or what may have happened to him would be extremely helpful. Xander had taken the liberty of exploring the house. It was supposed to be empty while being prepared for new exhibits and, to be honest, Xander looked most the part of someone in construction.

***

Shane nodded his head in agreement, but he had no idea what this woman was talking about. He had pegged her for the gossiping kind, so he approached her first to inquire about Felix. It had been a mistake. After twenty minutes of her making more flirtatious inquiries than giving him any pertinent information, Shane was reaching the limits of his patience. Luckily for him, another female student jumped into the conversation, and she was much more studious than the first one. Gretchen steered the conversation back toward the dig and what they had found. The other woman seemed to get bored with the conversation quickly now that it had taken a scholastic turn and excused herself.

"Like I was saying, Dr. Aiken may not have been super motivated as far as progress on the dig, but he taught us a lot otherwise. I just don't understand why he would just up and leave. Actually, I truly don't believe he would do that willingly, and I definitely don't understand him putting Declan in charge. Everyone knew they didn't get along in the least. Declan isn't very personable. He wasn't even here for the experience. He gave me more of a treasure hunter vibe than serious archeologist," Gretchen said, and Shane's interest was piqued.

"So, when was the last time you saw Dr. Aiken?" Shane asked, and she sighed.

"He usually kept to himself after the workday was over. The last time I saw him, we had convinced him to join us out at a pub the night before the room was discovered. Everyone was there, well except Declan, but no one minded—he was usually a drag. Dr. Aiken left early and in a hurry like he had forgotten an appointment or something. I only remember because he practically knocked me over on his way to the door," she said, and Shane nodded.

The other girl had also briefly mentioned something about a man named Declan. She hadn't seemed too impressed by him either. His hostility toward Felix, along with his new position, seemed a little suspect to Shane as well.

"Did Declan ever show up that night?" he asked, and she shook her head.

"No, but as I said, that wasn't really unusual for Declan. He always thought he was better than all of us and rarely hung out with anyone. He was too focused on finding buried treasure and hated Dr. Aiken for stalling him finding his fortune," she said.

Shane wanted to ask more questions, but Gretchen was called away by another student. He talked to a few more students but got pretty much the same information from all of them. They last saw Dr. Aiken at the pub the night before he disappeared. He had seemed calm but left in a hurry. Everyone was dumbfounded that he would leave Declan in charge and not say goodbye to anyone.

Shane went inside to find Declan but paused as a familiar scent tickled his nostrils. It was Molly's perfume. He followed the scent around the living room to a tapestry he knew hid a secret passage to the upstairs. Shane was just about to go into the passage when Xander entered the room with a young man. The man shot him a glare, and Xander's body language gave Shane all the information he needed.

The young man had to be Declan. He matched the description given to him by the other students, and he definitely was not human and not friendly. As much as Shane yearned to continue to follow Molly's scent, he knew that his opportunity was lost.

"I was just admiring this lovely piece of work," Shane said, knowing it was almost pointless to lie, but the man just nodded in acceptance and motioned for Shane to follow. Soon he and Xander were deposited back at the entrance, and Declan shut the front door behind them with a resounding thump. Xander and Shane exchanged looks before heading to the edge of the woods to find Claude. Claude shouldn't be too much longer.

* * *

Claude finally made it to the clearing, but there had been nothing in the hollow of the tree. This was not a good sign. Felix would never have just left without leaving some clue or word for them to follow or at least know that everything was okay. That knowledge had set Claude immediately on edge. He needed to get out of this dark wood before he lost control of the creeping feeling of dread that was coming over him. Claude had just stepped out of the clearing when he began to hear rustling and movement coming towards him.

"Declan, stop! What the hell is wrong with you? Let me go!" a female voice said angrily. It was a way away in the opposite direction of out, but Claude headed in that direction anyway. If Maura was truly back, then this woman could be in serious danger.

* * *

Gretchen pulled with all her might, but Declan was

stronger than she thought. He dragged her into the woods at the edge of the property, and she cursed herself for being so stupid. When Declan had approached her to discuss management of the dig, she thought that perhaps he had come to his senses. Since there obviously wasn't any monetary treasure to be found, she had hoped that he was leaving, or at least giving her control of the excavation. She had stupidly followed him away from the others.

Declan had never cared about other people's feelings, but Gretchen didn't want to discuss it in front of the other students. As soon as they were out of sight, he grabbed her roughly and practically dragged her into the woods. All the time she had spent in self-defense classes failed her in her struggle against him. If anything, she had only managed to drain her own energy, but she refused to give up. She refused to be a victim, not this time.

*　*　*

Gretchen had been a thorn in his side from day one. The way she fawned over Dr. Aiken was sickening, but now she would pay. She may have no idea what she had done, but he would make sure she suffered for it. He would give her to Maura. He was tired of hearing her complain about how she needed fresh, young blood, but first, Declan would have his own fun.

If only Gretchen knew how much he liked when women struggled against him. He was getting hard just thinking of the fight she would give him. Maybe he could convince Maura into letting him keep her as his slave. Maura could have a steady supply of blood, and he would have something to occupy himself with when Maura was dealing with the other three.

"Let me go!" Gretchen yelled, giving yet another tug, but he pulled her against him so that they were face to face.

"None of this would be happening if you had just kept your mouth shut," Declan growled, flashing his fangs at her.

He felt Gretchen tense in his arms, and he lost the last vestige of his control. Maura wouldn't mind if he had a sample of her first. Declan used her shock against her, releasing her just enough to position her more comfortably before he struck. Declan barely had the taste of her on his tongue before he was ripped away.

* * *

Claude had hoped he made it on time, but the sickening sound of tearing flesh as he pulled the man away told him otherwise. Claude was furious. He may have been too late to save her, but this guy was going to pay. Then he would question him.

It had been a while since Claude had been in a physical fight, so he was a little rusty, but the young man wasn't to full strength. Claude used that fact to his advantage, so it didn't take long for Claude to subdue him. If he hadn't heard the woman moan behind him, he would have continued to beat this new Vampire until his face was nothing more than a bloody pulp.

* * *

Gretchen lay stunned and in pain as she watched the most beautiful man she had ever seen beat the living daylights out of Declan. A part of her was glad he was getting punished for what he had done to her, but the rest of her was scared. She knew she was dying. She could feel the burning where the flesh on her neck had been ripped open. She could feel her blood pouring from her body, leaving her weak and hopeless. She only managed a gurgling moan of thanks before the world began to slip away.

* * *

Claude had no idea what came over him as he saw the woman's eyes gently flutter closed. They had been so sad, almost pleading as she had looked up at him. Even with her mangled neck, she looked strangely angelic. He knelt down beside her and bit into his wrist, letting his blood drip into her wound. He waited a few moments before licking his wound, sealing it.

He hoped she hadn't lost too much blood, as he noticed the puddle he was kneeling in was all hers. That was how the others found him. Kneeling in a puddle of the woman's blood, almost as if he were praying over her.

"What the hell happened here?" Xander demanded, lifting Claude up from his collar and away from the woman.

"I went to the tree, and there was nothing, but as I was heading out of the woods, I heard her screaming. I raced towards her voice just as that man over there was about to bite her," Claude said, pointing to where Declan's battered body had lain.

Their eyes followed his half gesture, but instead of the mangled body they expected, there was nothing but a few droplets of blood and drag marks. Claude blinked a few times just to be sure that he saw it correctly. How long had he been kneeling over the woman? He should have heard him getting away at the least.

"She's healing! Claude, what did you do?" Shane said, standing over the woman.

Xander dropped Claude and bent over her, inspecting her neck.

"You turned her?" Xander asked, obviously upset, and Claude cursed.

"It was instinct. I just couldn't let her die. Not like that," he said, and Shane shook his head.

"I'm going to follow these drag marks," Shane grumbled and marched off in the direction they led.

* * *

Xander glared at Claude for a moment before his face softened. Claude had never had the greatest impulse control, and, judging from the way they had found him standing so protectively over the woman, Xander had a feeling that this, like the turning of Cat, was somehow fated to happen. This woman could be a phoenix waiting for its time to rise from the ashes.

"Take her back to the hotel. Shane and I will find this guy," he said and gave Claude a pat on the shoulder.

CHAPTER FOURTEEN

Shane followed the tracks all the way to the edge of the woods, but that was where they disappeared. From there, he tried to pick up on the scent, but it was no use. The smell was that of Declan, and since he practically lived on the estate, it was everywhere. He silently cursed Claude for letting that bastard getaway. Leave it to Claude to get all wayward in the presence of a woman. Shane decided to head back up to the house.

It was already getting dark, and most of the students from earlier were gone. Declan wouldn't have had any problem getting past them without being seen, even injured. Declan would, however, need shelter to heal, and it gave Shane an excuse to look for whatever had given off Molly's scent.

* * *

Molly's emotions were at war as she saw Shane approaching the house from her office window. She still loved him, even though he had left her to die, but the man approaching the house didn't look like the man she had remembered. He also didn't seem like a man enjoying life. His shoulders were hunched, and his expression was grim. He no longer walked with a bounce in his step, and it made Molly wonder if maybe she had been a bit rash to jump to conclusions about what had happened that night.

Molly's thoughts were interrupted by yelling down the

hall. Maura didn't do yelling, so something had to be majorly wrong.

"You imbecile! I should kill you now!" Maura yelled, and Molly flinched. This was definitely not good.

"I got away, and the one who attacked me didn't know who I was. Besides, I was trying to do something nice for you. You are always complaining about not being able to kill Molly. Gretchen would have been a perfect solution. You would get the young blood you so desperately crave, and I would get something to play with since I can't touch Molly either," Declan said.

His words were slurred and gurgled as if he were talking with a mouth full of spit and no lips. Molly's stomach began to churn with disgust. She didn't want to hear any more, but she had to know what the hell was going on.

"Am I that distasteful to you? You ungrateful sack of shit!" Maura yelled.

Declan chuckled, or Molly thought he chuckled. He could be choking—she wasn't sure. One thing Molly was sure about, Maura and Declan were not the people she thought they were. They were not good people. She had suspected that, but she made allowances since they had saved her. They helped her survive losing everyone and everything she had loved, but now she knew that they had their own agenda, and Molly wasn't sure she wanted to be a part of it.

Making up her mind, Molly grabbed her purse from the back of her chair and began forming an escape plan. Declan had always been in control of her dealings with the outside world, but she knew where he had a stash of cash in the apartment. She just needed to get back there without Declan and

Maura figuring out she wasn't at the estate. Maybe she could slip away while they were still arguing.

Molly's plan was already in motion. She no longer needed them, and she wasn't going to let them drag her into whatever mess they were in. Unfortunately, leaving their mess behind meant finding her own answers, and to be honest, Molly wasn't so sure she was up to the task. However, it wasn't like she really had a choice. Staying with those two was definitely a death sentence. Molly slipped out of the house undetected, to her relief. It was already pretty dark, so no one would see her crossing the massive lawn away from the estate.

* * *

Shane was torn as he saw a figure with a striking resemblance to Molly scampering across the lawn away from the house. He had only just got inside, and the arguing upstairs was of more importance right now. For all he knew, he could be hallucinating again. The others had no idea, but since Molly's death, Shane had started experimenting with drugs again. At first, he passed it off as just continuing his research with a new twist, but now he was fully aware that it had become an addiction.

When he was high, he could see Molly whenever he wanted, which was why he had rarely been sober since. Except for now—he hadn't been able to bring his drugs with him on this trip. Besides, if he was going to be fighting Maura again, he needed to be in his right mind, but that didn't mean his past usage or withdrawal symptoms weren't having lingering effects. Shane shook his head and continued to the stairs. If

Molly was out there, he would find her, but for now, he had to find out what happened to his friend.

* * *

Claude paced the hotel room. Xander and Shane had returned with very unsettling news.

"Empty? How could the house be empty?" Claude asked when they all regrouped at the hotel.

"I know! I heard them arguing, but by the time I got upstairs, they were gone," Shane said, and Xander nodded.

"I was right behind him. I didn't see anyone leave, and we searched the house together afterward. All the passages and rooms were empty," Xander said, and Claude cursed.

"So, did we find out anything about Felix at least?" Claude said, and both Shane and Xander's faces were grim.

"Maura's tomb wasn't as empty as we thought. There were no recognizable pieces of Felix left, but his body was all over the room. I hate to say it, but Maura is most definitely back, and I think this Declan character is her newest pet," Xander said, and Claude groaned. This was definitely not good.

"I'll schedule for us to fly back tomorrow," Shane said and left for his own room. Xander nodded and went back to his.

He wanted to call and check on Cat. With Maura on the loose and on the run, he didn't trust her at the house alone. He needed to warn her.

Cat answered on the first ring as if she had been waiting by the phone for his call.

"Cat, we will be home in a day or two, but things here didn't go well," Xander began, but Cat cut him off.

"What? Is anyone hurt? Are you hurt? What about Molly? Maura?" she rambled, but he sighed, stopping her.

"Our friend Felix is dead, and we are sure Maura is alive and has the help of a man named Declan. I want you to be extra careful until we get back. No going out. Don't answer the door for anyone period. I really need you to be safe until I can get back to you," Xander said, and his tone was all business.

"You've got a deal. And Xander?" she stalled, unsure if she should even broach this topic right now.

"Yes, Cat," he urged.

"We have a lot to talk about when you get back, okay?" she said, and he chuckled.

"Of course," Xander said and hung up.

No matter what else was going on, he would make time to have a talk with Cat. This week had proven to him that he couldn't wait for Cat to decide she was ready. He had to make sure she knew she belonged to him now.

* * *

Cat smiled to herself as she hung up. She was excited to have them coming home, even if she now also had to be on the lookout for Maura and this Declan guy. Things had finally begun to feel normal again after her late-night visitation. Cat still wasn't entirely sure it had been real and not a dream, but then again, her dreams were seemingly real if the necklace on her neck was any indication.

CHAPTER FIFTEEN

Cat sat drinking breakfast when there was a knock at the door. She had no intentions of answering, but she was at least curious to see who had made it to the doorstep with all the added security around. She really hoped it wasn't that creepy ghost again. She was pretty sure it was Rachel's spirit. It only made sense that Xander's ex would haunt her. Cat's heart nearly stopped when she saw Molly standing there looking more than haggard. Despite every warning bell going off inside her, Cat opened the door.

"Hello Catherine," Molly said, but her tone sounded forced. This wasn't the Molly that Cat remembered, and it surely wasn't the Molly from her dreams. Molly's eyes studied Cat, and she visibly paled upon seeing the necklace around her neck.

"How did you get that?" Molly stammered.

Cat narrowed her eyes. So maybe this was the Molly from her dreams.

"How do you know about the necklace?" Cat asked, and she saw Molly's shoulder slump.

"I'm so sorry," Molly whispered before she began to sob.

As angry as Cat was with her at that moment, Molly was her best friend. No matter what had happened over the last three years, they would get past it. Cat wrapped her arms around Molly, leading her into the house. Xander would get over the fact that she was going against everything she had just promised him.

There was no way she was going to let Molly just walk away again. For starters, Cat had a million questions for her. Then there was the matter of Shane. He would never forgive her if she let Molly walk out of their lives now.

"Why don't I go first, since you are pulling yourself together?" Cat said, and Molly nodded.

"I saw your head severed from your body. There was no way for Shane to bring you back. We both have grieved for you for so long. If we had known there was a way, we both would have moved heaven and earth to do so," Cat said, but Molly frowned.

"My head was gone? No wonder it took me weeks to talk after I woke up. Declan said Shane told you I was dead and that you didn't question it," she said, and Cat frowned.

Wasn't Declan the one helping Maura?

"Wait, how do you know Declan?" Cat asked, and Molly sighed.

"He was the one who saved me—well, Maura too. She was the one who gave me that necklace and taught me how to use spells to send you that dream," Molly said, and Cat couldn't help her instant reaction to move away from Molly.

"Shane never told you about Maura?" Cat asked.

Molly frowned and shook her head.

"Maura told me he betrayed her. She saved him from certain death, and he returned the favor by trying to kill her," she said.

Cat shook her head. The change had obviously not cured Molly of her trusting nature.

"I don't know the whole story. I will admit that, but one thing I do know is that Shane is not like that, and neither are Xander and Claude. Seriously, Molly, this is what I meant all those years about you being so gullible," Cat said, and Molly had to laugh.

Cat hadn't changed as much as Molly had believed. They spent the rest of the night laughing and joking, just like the old times. They both didn't want to dwell on the bad stuff, at least not that night.

* * *

Xander was so excited to get home to Cat that he almost missed the extra presence in the house. His senses were on red alert as he made his way inside.

"Cat!" Xander called as soon as he came into the door.

"Xander!" Cat called back with all the attitude he had come to expect from her over the years.

He headed in the direction of her voice, but he was still on the lookout. Cat may be fine, but that didn't mean the other person in the house wasn't a threat. He signaled for Shane and Claude to wait outside with Gretchen until he could locate Cat and get her out of the house. Whoever this person was, he planned on finding them without putting anyone else in any further danger.

* * *

Molly sat tensely next to Cat as they awaited Xander. Molly wasn't sure that she was ready to face the others, but Cat had insisted she stay. Xander burst through the door and was only a few steps from Cat when he paused and glared at

Molly. The fires of anger burning in his eyes as he glared at her didn't help Molly's fear. She had known he wouldn't be as welcoming as Cat had said they would be, but Molly could only have hoped. Xander grabbed Cat roughly against him, daring Molly with his eyes to make any sort of movement.

"Xander, it's not what you think," Cat said, and he turned his glare on her instead.

"She almost killed you," he snarled.

Cat rolled her eyes and pushed herself out of his grasp.

"Molly is my best friend. She didn't understand what was going on. She's not evil, and she's staying with us," Cat said.

She crossed her arms over her chest, daring him to challenge her decision.

"She is not staying," he growled, and Cat raised an eyebrow at him.

"Then I won't be either, and to think I was going to tell you I love you," Cat said, marching over to Molly.

She grabbed Molly's hand and proceeded to drag her out of the room and toward the front door. They only made it as far as the hall before Cat was ripped away from Molly and deposited firmly against Xander. She could feel him shaking with unspoken rage, but instead of a verbal tongue lashing, he bent down stealing, any protest she could have had in a soul melting kiss.

* * *

Molly turned away, being forced to stand awkwardly nearby while her friend was getting carried away with Xander. Molly couldn't say she was surprised that those two had gotten together. The night she died, Molly had hoped Shane would bring Xander instead of Claude. The date may have been a lot less interesting, but it just may have avoided her untimely demise. Oh, and her nearly killing her best friend in some stupid revenge spell. Molly bit her lip thinking about how gullible she had been. This was her second chance, well, her third chance, but she was going to make it count.

* * *

Shane sat tensely in the car. He knew Molly was inside, but he would wait for Xander's signal. Right now, he needed to stay with Claude and Gretchen. She still hadn't awakened, and Claude sat nervously beside her corpselike body. This scene was a little too close for comfort, but he would just have to deal with it. Besides, it was quite amusing to see the way Claude was already doting on the woman. From the brief encounter Shane had had with Gretchen before her brush with death, he knew she was way too practical a woman to take Claude seriously. Maybe she would help him finally grow up.

After sitting in the car for what felt like hours, Shane finally saw movement by the door. He sat up and got out of the car to investigate, only to stop short. There in the doorway was Molly. His heart skipped a beat as his body moved without his brain's consent. In seconds he had her in his arms, his face poised to kiss the lips he had dreamed of so often for so long now. Molly was alive, and she was here, and she would finally be his.

* * *

Molly almost let herself get swept up in the emotions flooding her body. She so desperately wanted to complete the kiss that was sure to come if she did nothing to stop it, but she was going to stop it. Molly was serious about not being so gullible this time around. She pushed herself out of his grasp and slapped him, leaving him stunned and confused.

"How dare you touch me?" Molly said, finding a new wealth of anger.

So maybe he hadn't really left her for dead. Their love had been real, too real, so real that he should have stopped at nothing to be with her. He should have guarded her grave so that monster of a woman couldn't turn her against him and her best friend. He hadn't been devoted enough, and Molly wasn't so sure she could go down that road with him again.

***

Claude fought a chuckle as he watched the drama unfolding on the front steps. Molly was indeed back, but she definitely wasn't the same woman. That was a perk for Claude, but obviously not a good sign for Shane. His dear friend had a lot of begging to do before she would forgive him. It's always the romantics that get burned, which is why he was decidedly not one of those sappy fools.

Claude felt movement against his leg, and his attention jerked back to the woman beside him. She was the second woman he had turned. Yet his reaction to her was far different than his reaction to Cat. Maybe this one woman was the answer to the prayer he never dared to speak aloud. The woman who was most dangerous to him and his way of life, possibly even more dangerous than Maura herself.

CHAPTER SIXTEEN

The air in the room was heavy with tension as everyone sat around the study, just looking at each other. Molly was glaring at Shane, who stared longingly at her. Cat refused to look at Xander while he glared at her for being so stubborn. Claude, well, he watched all of them, feeding on their drama to help distract him from thoughts of the woman lying unconscious in the bedroom right next to his. Any attempt at talking out the situation at hand had quickly turned into a shouting match with lots of pointed fingers and no real solutions.

Cat and Shane wanted Molly to stay. Xander was adamantly opposed to it, and Claude just wanted to check on Gretchen. From his brief time knowing old Molly, he didn't think she would harm a fly. After time spent under the thumb of Maura and the way she was glaring at Shane, Claude was sure the old Molly wasn't who they were dealing with.

She had lost some of her innocence. With that, Claude knew that nothing with her would ever be simple again. He felt bad for Shane but saw no way to help him in what was bound to be a long journey to reconciliation.

"This situation is not ideal. I would rather not be here, but at the moment I have no other place to go," Molly said, finally taking her glare from Shane and settling it on Xander.

"I can't have you here. You are a threat to all of us," Xander said, which had Cat and Shane visibly bristling.

"I don't see how this is even a discussion. It was our fault she ended up in the hands of Maura. She is no more a threat to us than a warm breeze. Molly, you are staying," Cat declared before storming out of the room.

Xander just stood there for a moment watching the door Cat stormed out of. Claude fought back a smile as he saw Xander's jaw muscle twitch. The honeymoon phase had been even shorter than Claude had anticipated. Cat was a very strong-willed woman, and Xander—well—Xander was practically a caveman when it came to modern women. Hence, it was more of an amusement than a surprise.

"This conversation is not over, but for tonight you can stay," Xander ground out before stalking out of the room after Cat.

The man was definitely on a mission.

"The nerve," Molly huffed before leaving the room as well.

"Molly, wait! We still need to talk," Shane called, following after her.

The arguing ensued, and Claude shook his head. With those four now occupied, he finally had a chance to see to Gretchen.

* * *

"How dare he!" Cat fumed to herself as she paced her room.

Xander had some nerve to try to kick Molly out of the house. So, what if she had sent Cat that horrible dream? It had been a mistake, and after Molly explained, Cat couldn't blame her for being angry. She had been woken from the dead, only to find that her true love had abandoned her and turned her best friend. Not to mention, she had been tricked by Maura. Maura had managed to keep Claude, Shane, and Xander under her spell for years, and not to be mean, but Molly was very trusting.

How could he hold it against her? Then to make matters worse, he'd acted all caveman, like she was his property or something. One night of amazing sex did not make her his. In the middle of her musings, there was a knock at her door. She knew who it had to be, and she was just itching to give him a piece of her mind.

"What do you want, Xander?" Cat asked, and he pulled her against him.

"I want you," he said, kissing her neck. He kicked the door closed behind him.

She pushed away from him, putting space between their bodies. Cat wasn't a fool. She knew her body wouldn't allow her to get her point across if she let him touch her. Just to be safe, she gave him her back, not trusting even to look in his direction. To think, she had allowed a little sex and danger trick her heart into falling in love.

* * *

Xander wasn't going to let her pull away from him, especially not now. The thought of something happening to her had nearly killed him. When he realized she hadn't been alone in the house, he had nearly lost it. Cat may not understand why he was so suspicious of Molly, but that was no reason to shut him out completely. She couldn't possibly understand the extent of Maura's evil.

For all they knew, this could be a trap. Molly could be a spy sent to destroy them from within. She had spent enough time with Maura to be fully under her spell, and well, she couldn't hide her hatred for Shane. Despite the situation, it didn't change the fact that Cat was his, and sooner rather than later, he would make her realize that.

Xander turned Cat to face him. Looking into her eyes, he saw the fight building in them and smirked. He knew she wanted him just as much as he wanted her, but she was still fighting what was between them. She may be upset about it, but Xander had every intention of proving to her that she was his and his alone for the rest of eternity. Xander was staking his claim here and now. He kissed her, letting all the emotion within him seep into his movements. His mouth moved against hers until her lips parted with a sigh. Xander wasn't going to let this moment of surrender escape him.

* * *

This time Cat didn't fight him, couldn't fight what she was feeling. Not that she had ever really fought the attraction between them once she'd had that first taste. She just let go, and it wasn't long before Cat found herself naked in bed with him. He took his time exploring her body with his hands and mouth as if he didn't want to miss touching or kissing any inch of flesh. He took particularly good care to thoroughly explore between her legs with his tongue. Cat had never experienced anything as erotic as the feel of his fangs grazing her clit as he devoured her in her most sensitive of areas.

"Xander, please," Cat begged, pushing at his shoulders.

As much as Cat would have loved to have him continue, she wanted him inside her, to claim her the way his eyes had promised before they had even begun. Xander chuckled, ignoring her plea and nipping at her clit, causing her to buck against him. He was enjoying hearing her beg for him. He wanted to give in, but the urge to make her come against his mouth was stronger.

Xander was making it clear that he was the one in control of her body, and as intriguing as it was, Cat needed to let him know that she had some control over this as well. She grabbed his hair, pulling him up so she could kiss him. Her hands drifted down his sculpted chest to rub his throbbing erection. Xander's groan let her know that, indeed, the tables had been turned. Xander's hips began to move, his throbbing member pumping into her hands, mimicking the movement of their tongues. She felt him jump before he stilled in her hands.

Apparently, Xander was having a little issue with controlling his own body, which made Cat grin. She loved that she had that much power over him. Xander was the picture of control in everyday life, and she enjoyed the thought of being able to change that about him. Cat didn't want to waste any more time with power plays.

Her body was screaming for release from all the sexual tension. Guiding him to her dripping entrance, she slid Xander inside of her inch by glorious inch. He was hot, hard, and oh, so perfect as he filled her. Cat felt a sense of completion as they lay for a moment, just enjoying the feel of being connected in the most intimate of ways.

* * *

Xander gritted his teeth as he allowed for Cat's body to adjust to his size. The gentle squeeze of her inner muscles as it accommodated him was nearly his undoing. He cursed himself for letting her get the upper hand and bringing him to this point. He had to think of something else to keep from embarrassing himself. Xander was not some kid, and this was not his first time with a woman. He should control himself, but then again, this wasn't just any woman; this was Cat.

From day one, she had managed to break his façade of calm at any moment. She was more to him than he could ever have imagined. Cat bucked her hips against him, dragging him out of his thoughts and back to reality. Back to the threat of making what he had planned to be a long night of staking his claim into a short bout of lustful rutting.

He began to move his hips in a slow circular motion, making Cat gasp in surprise as pleasure instantly started to build within her. It felt so amazing. It was like she had never experienced the pleasure of sex before. He maintained a slow, torturous pace, sliding in and out of her. A pace that would have made the tortoise look like the hare if they were racing. This was not merely sex, but a joining of two souls, and Cat knew then that there would never be any denying that she was his and he was hers.

This wasn't about who had more power or control in the relationship; this was about being together as one. Each was a part of the other. With one final swivel, Xander and Cat came apart in each other's arms, and it was like nothing either of them had ever experienced before. It had shaken the very foundation of who Cat had thought she had been or ever could be regarding Xander and vice versa.

When the last waves of pleasure subsided, and the reality came sweeping in, Xander held Cat close, kissing her brow gently. He was afraid that once they fully came down from the high of their lovemaking that she would push him away again, and he just couldn't stomach that idea.

"Marry me?" he asked, and Cat smiled.

"Are you sure you haven't lost your mind?" Cat asked, and he laughed.

"It was lost the day you came into my life," he said.

Cat had to roll her eyes, but then she smiled and kissed him.

"Then, yes! I'll marry you, but first, I need to make sure everything is straight with Molly. I don't want us getting in the way of making sure she doesn't end up back with Maura," Cat said, and he frowned.

"You know I won't let that happen," Xander said, and she smiled.

"I know you will try your best," Cat said.

"I refuse to discuss this any further tonight. Right now, I intend to spend the rest of the night enjoying the bounty of your flesh," he growled, pinning her to the bed with his massive body.

* * *

Cat knew exactly what he was about to do, and so she beat him to it. She sank her teeth into his neck just where it met his shoulders and drank from him.

Xander's whole body shook as pleasure flooded his body,

and Cat felt him grow hard against her leg. Xander had known that there would be a pleasure when bitten by a female Vampire. Still, given that his only experience had been with Maura, he hadn't realized how pleasurable it could actually be. He was very intrigued to see how much it would enhance their lovemaking.

"You're mine," Xander growled before plunging not only his newfound erection into Cat but his fangs into her neck.

Cat reached orgasm immediately at this new double penetration and was overwhelmed by the duration and intensity of it all. She could very well get used to this.

CHAPTER SEVENTEEN

"I can't believe Xander actually talked you into this?" Shane teased Cat as he walked her down the aisle. She was stunning in her off-white, mermaid style wedding gown. Even the dreaded ghost necklace did nothing to diminish her bridal glow.

"Shut up before I trip and ruin my dress," Cat said through clenched teeth.

The wedding ceremony was small, but Xander had spared no expense. The courtyard of the house was covered with white satin and lace and flowers. He made sure everything was perfect for when he made Cat his. Xander had always been one for upholding tradition. Shane did his best to hide his reaction when his gaze collided with Molly's, who was standing as Cat's Maid of Honor.

If only things had been different, they could have had the same. Molly was no longer his Molly; she was her own being, and it ate at him continuously because it was his own doing. He would find a way to get her back. He knew he would.

* * *

Molly did her best to focus her attention solely on her best friend as the man she used to love walked her down the aisle. As much as Molly tried to focus on Cat today, it was hard not to feel depressed. If things had gone the way they should have, it would have been Molly in the white dress with Cat standing where Molly was. It would have been Shane waiting impatiently at the end of the aisle for Molly to be brought to him. They would have said their vows in front of friends and lived happily together forever.

Instead, she had been decapitated and raised from the dead by evil Vampires. She had been tricked into almost killing her best friend, and now here she was. She wasn't her old self, and everyone knew that, but for today, she would pretend. She had to, for Cat. It was the least she could do.

* * *

Cat looked down the aisle at Xander and couldn't help the tears welling in her eyes. Cat wasn't the one who usually got teary over weddings. Then again, she had never thought her wedding would be something this beautiful. As kids, Molly always joked that Cat would have drunkenly gotten married in Vegas to a total stranger, and well, Cat had thought about the same thing. She would have never expected she would fall in love with a gorgeous warrior turned Vampire. She was not the typical lead in fairy tale romances, and yet here she was, walking down the aisle toward her true love with tears of joy in her eyes.

* * *

Xander was fighting back his own tears as Cat made her way down the aisle toward him. She looked every inch the blushing bride, and Xander couldn't wait to have her alone, as his wife. Cat might have protested this ceremony at first, but Xander knew it was necessary. There had been too much drama too soon in their relationship. Not to mention the planning of the ceremony had gotten everyone's minds off the fact that Maura and Declan were still at large. They had disappeared without a trace, and Xander knew that in no way was this a reprieve. When Maura and Declan did surface again, it wasn't going to be without an army behind them. When that day came, Xander had every intention of being just as prepared with an army of his own. For now, he was focused on only one thing: his bride.

* * *

Claude held his breath to combat the giant yawn building in his throat. As beautiful as everything was, in his mind, it was completely unnecessary. Xander had been claiming Cat all over the house for weeks now. You would think that Xander would have given up on the more antiquated traditions like this, but apparently not. Besides, if it were truly a traditional ceremony, then technically, it should have been him giving away the bride. Being her sire kind of made her his daughter. One he would never have asked for, but she had his blood in her, so that made them related. The only interesting part of the whole wedding was watching Gretchen trying to pretend she wasn't into this sappy love fest. He couldn't seem to keep his eyes off of her, even as she began to cry when Xander and Cat said their vows. Claude hated weeping women, but for her, he would make an exception.

About the Author Stella Williams

Stella Williams is a Blogger and USA TODAY Bestselling Paranormal Romance & Urban Fantasy Author, who lives in Washington State. She has a degree in Anthropology from The University of California, Santa Cruz. Stella prides herself in using her studies to create diverse worlds and characters for her novels. You can find more about Stella Williams on her website: www.serpentinecreative.com

Keep up to date with Stella Williams and her latest projects.

https://serpentinecreative.com/getsocial/

Want More of Stella's Seductive Supernatural World?
Explore Stella's Catalogue

https://serpentinecreative.com/getbooks

Continue reading for an excerpt of

Ferocious

Secret of Ceres Book 1

Full Moon

Daphne climbed from her bedroom window and onto the landing of the fire escape. She paused as it creaked under her weight. She started sneaking out three months ago and knew it would hold her weight, just not how long.

The apartment building where she and her family lived survived on sheer will alone. The elevators hardly ever worked, the stairwell reeked of urine and weed smoke. No one cared what anyone around them did. Everyone stuck to themselves regardless of the situation. The perfect environment outside of Ceres for a family of Aura to go unnoticed. The easiest place to hide from the outside world while still living and navigating within it.

Her family could afford better. Fear and proximity to Ceres kept them stuck in this hell hole. Daphne dreamed of living without fear. Lots of Aura teens who grew up outside of the Great Sanctuary of Ceres felt the way she did. They didn't want to choose between the freedom of the outside world and the freedom to use their gifts. They wanted both. On nights like this, they defied the rules by gathering to practice their energy knowledge without limitation. The Resistance, they called themselves, organized and fought for the freedom to be themselves. At least from what the brochure said. Daphne found The Resistance mostly blogged about social injustices around the world and partied at the local hot spot, Club Obelisk.

The full moon beckoned, filling her with excited energy. Daphne rushed down the metal ladder using her Aura energy to sense the way in the pitch black of the alleyway. The buildings stood tall enough to block any of the moon's magnificent light from reaching its secrets. The only other source of light in the alley had long been broken, and no one cared to fix it.

"Took you long enough," James said, startling Daphne.

She smiled and launched herself into his waiting arms. Daphne and James flirted for a month now, and she hoped that maybe this evening made things official.

"Benji wouldn't fall asleep. I had to wait him out," Daphne whispered.

He took her mouth in a passionate kiss. They made out in the dark until a sharp whistle cut through the silent night air, time to go. The others wouldn't wait for them much longer. James took Daphne's hand and led her out of the alley to a waiting van. Tonight, was a special night. They wouldn't be joining The Resistance at Club Obelisk. It was their first official date—a house party being thrown somewhere on the outskirts of town. While Daphne preferred that they travel to the party just the two of them, she couldn't be any more excited.

"Hurry up. They are waiting," the driver said.

He looked back at them through the rearview mirror. Daphne never met these boys before. Human, but not part of The Resistance. She knew all ten of the human members there, James included. It made Daphne nervous. She studied James' energy. Finding him to be calm and excited, she snuggled closer to him.

"Let's go, then. Wouldn't want to keep them waiting," James said.

His voice sounded deeper than usual. Like he wanted to project a manly façade in front of his friends.

"Who's all going to be there? Will there be anyone I know," Daphne asked.

James smiled at her and shook his head.

"No one you know. I want you to get to know a different set of friends.

I'm sure once you meet them, you'll understand," James said.

Daphne ignored the warning bells going off in her head. James acted like a different person, but that's what humans did. They changed personalities based on the situation. Daphne could understand that, living her life as an Aura in the outside world. Still, Daphne couldn't shake the gnawing feeling in her stomach.

She shifted in her seat. Her senses picked up on a delicate swirl of dark energy. They drove farther and farther from the city. Her palms began to sweat, and her stomach started to twist in knot—the air heavy with ill intent.

"Pull over!" Daphne snapped as they reached the last few blocks of civilization.

James' friends chuckled, and he wrapped a tight arm around her waist.

"Chill out, babe. We've got big plans for you tonight."

The implication of his words sent Daphne into a panic. She focused on the vehicle's engine, feeling out its energy until she found just the right component to manipulate. The car sputtered and began to smoke before the engine died. As soon as it slowed, Daphne lunged for the door. She almost made it out van before James grabbed her by the ankles.

"I thought I told you to neutralize her before she got in the van," the driver shouted.

She struggled with all her might.

"I did! I slipped her the potion while we kissed," James snapped.

Daphne screamed and kicked for dear life as they pulled her back into the van. She prayed for someone, anyone to hear and come to her rescue. She missed her chance.

"Guess I'll do it the old-fashioned way. Boss is going to be pissed," the other boy from the van said.

A big black object came flying at Daphne's face. The force of someone's fist impacting her jaw sent her flying into the wall of the van. She heard the sickening sound of flesh connecting with flesh before her head hit the metal behind her. Everything went black.

Ferocious
A Steamy & Suspenseful OwnVoices Paranormal Romance
Available Now
www.serpentinecreative.com/getbooks

www.ingramcontent.com/pod-product-compliance
Ingram Content Group UK Ltd.
Pitfield, Milton Keynes, MK11 3LW, UK
UKHW041412180426
11947UKWH00007B/80